THE ODD COUPLE

By

G.A.HAUSER

G. A. HAUSER

THE ODD COUPLE

Prologue

Marty Hayes rubbed his clammy palms on his trouser legs. He was in a conference room in a downtown LA law office. He felt awkward and numb and wasn't sure why he was here.

Marty glanced up at the door to the conference room, seeing a man around his own age, twenty-five, maybe twenty-six. The young man appeared scruffy with an unshaven jaw, messy hair, worn jeans, and a shabby T-shirt.

A woman of color entered the room, holding a file of paperwork. "Why don't you two take a seat," she said, setting the file down at the head of the table.

Marty tugged at the cuffs of his starched shirt, then adjusted the collar nervously. He glanced at the young man in the casual clothing.

They avoided each other's stares.

~

Kelsie O'Loughlin didn't know why he had been notified to come here. The call from this attorney's office confused him.

Out of curiosity, he made the drive to this downtown highrise in lousy Friday evening traffic.

As he looked at the other man in the room, Kelsie wondered if he was as befuddled as himself.

The pretty lawyer in the blazer and skirt held an envelope. "Thank you for coming. My name is Sonja Knight, and I've been instructed to read the last will and testament of Benjy Louis Lloyd." She opened a sealed envelope and slipped papers out of it, putting on a pair of designer eyeglasses.

Kelsie had no idea he was in Benjy's will. He was more than a little surprised. He rested his forearms on the table and interlaced his fingers.

Thoughts of Benjy, of his kindness and generosity washed over him.

THE ODD COUPLE

~

Marty stared at his fingernails as the anticipation began to build. Why Benjy had left him anything at all was puzzling. He adored the older man, but wasn't sure why he'd been included. Maybe Benjy had left other things to family members. They never spoke about it while they were together.

He perked up when the Ms Knight addressed him.

"What I have in front of me is the final will, one that had been updated three weeks ago." She fanned through pages and began to read.

While she did, Marty zoned off at the legal jargon. He tried to keep alert, listening for his name, and imagined sweet Benjy giving him a token gift.

"And…" Sonja Knight read, "The estate in Beverly Hills, the property Mr Lloyd occupied until his death, as well the total sum of his personal bank accounts are to be divided between the two of you as long as you meet the conditions."

Marty met gazes with the young man sitting across from him and neither of them said a word.

As she ended the reading of Benjy's will, Ms Knight handed each man a sealed envelope. "He requested that I give these to you. The settlement is based on a contingency. The details of the contract are included in the paperwork."

Marty took his and held it to his chest.

"Congratulations to you both. I have a few contracts for you to sign and then we're done."

Taking the pen from her hand, Marty tried to get over the shock. It had come out of the blue, like Benjy's death.

Chapter 1

In a cheap motel, Kelsie lay back on his single bed, blowing out the smoke from his mouth. He held the joint up to look at it, feeling a light headiness from the strong weed. He squashed it out in a tiny coaster beside him, and thought about what had happened earlier this evening.

It remained a puzzle.

Kelsie reached for his guitar, scooted higher on the bed, and strummed a few chords.

As he wrapped his head around the idea of living in a mansion and not having to play music for handouts, he stared into space.

Though Benjy had indeed helped him out when he was at his lowest, this act of kindness amazed him.

It would be nice to never have to go hungry again.

He picked up the letter Benjy had written, and gazed at his scrolling handwriting. The line that stuck out the most was, 'Please be happy.'

Kelsie wondered why Benjy had paired him off with an unlikely housemate. But, Benjy Lloyd had one mean sense of humor.

~

Marty packed. He filled each new cardboard box with select items using a label maker and marking pen on the top. He wrote, 'Clothing from top drawer of dresser' on one, then folded the lid and taped it.

THE ODD COUPLE

Making perfectly stacked rows, Marty had nearly all his personal items loaded.

As he carefully hand-wrapping glasses, Marty wondered if he should donate his household items to charity. He knew Benjy's home had everything he needed, and more.

That home. That enormous mansion with the pool, nine bedrooms, thirteen bathrooms...

If Benjy had any family left alive, Marty imagined they'd battle him for what he was given. Marty wasn't sure what had transpired, but the conditions to the will did surprise him.

"Oh, well." Marty shrugged and finished wrapping the glasses.

~

While parked in his car, Kelsie paused to stare at the home.

It was set back from the street and surrounded by an iron gate. He dug into his pocket and removed items given to him by the lawyer; a few keys, credit and debit cards, pass-codes, and remote clickers. He pointed one at the gate. It slowly opened, as if ghosts were dragging it backwards.

He parked his car and then hauled his guitar and a duffle-bag out of the trunk. Kelsie hoisted his bag to his shoulder and walked up the paved drive to the mansion's main entrance.

The home was maintained by a host of landscapers, pool and house cleaners, as well as a married couple who did the cooking and day to day chores.

He had told Benjy in jest, the man didn't even have to wipe his own bottom if he didn't want to.

It had made Benjy laugh.

Kelsie stared at the front of the home, the two floors, with terraces surrounding the upper bedroom windows.

This experience was surreal and felt as if he had fallen into either a rabbit hole or a lousy sit-com.

He expected someone to fight the decision. Was there really no one left of Benjy's family?

How could Benjy change his will this way? For him? He'd never asked the man for a dime although, Benjy had helped him out... a lot.

Standing on the front steps, Kelsie looked up at a camera which aimed his way. He waved, being silly, and then dug his fingers back into his worn jean pockets for a key.

Since he had several, including keys to a Bentley and a Maserati, Kelsie took a moment to find the correct one. The lawyer or someone else who had been considerate, had placed tiny ID tags on them.

He set his guitar and bag down, opening his palm and going through the keys. He tried one in the lock and it worked, opening the door.

He pushed it back and stood still, taking in the size of the foyer and the opulence.

"This is a trip, dude."

~

Marty drove his old Prius ahead of a small rental van. He had typed up an email to his apartment manager that he was moving out, gave back his keys and parking permit, and filled out a change of address card at the post office.

Pulling up to the iron gate, Marty picked up a remote control and pointed it. The gate moved back.

He waited, seeing the van in his rearview mirror and then proceeded up to the front of the mansion. Once he put his car in park, Marty went over the list he had made of where he wanted each of his boxes to go.

He had a printout from the computer of the floor plan.

He met with the van driver, who had one companion to help him, at the front door. He stuck his key in and opened it. "Okay.

Here's where everything needs to go." He gave them the printout.

"Got it." His list was taken and the van was opened from the back.

Marty stood in the impressive entryway, admiring the hand-blown glass chandelier and the white marble flooring.

A grand staircase wound its way to the second floor, and the men carried his boxes of clothing to the master bedroom.

The lawyer's paperwork in hand, Marty walked through the main hall to the kitchen, seeing how spotless it had been kept. He set his items on the table and noticed ingredients to make a margarita, as well as a sticky spill left on the counter.

He picked up a sponge and mopped it up, then noticed the sliding back door was open. After wiping off his hand, he approached the glass.

Someone was lying on a raft in the pool, sunglasses on, wearing a bathing suit, holding a drink in his hand, floating in the sunshine.

Marty stepped out of the kitchen and had a look around. A pitcher of green liquid was resting on the glass and iron table in the shade of an umbrella and a box of crackers had been opened, the contents dumped into a little pile.

He walked closer to the edge of the immaculate pool. "When did you get here?"

"Later, dude. Don't kill the buzz."

Marty pivoted on the balls of his leather soles and stepped back into the house. He slid the door closed, and spotted the movers waiting for him. After taking out his checkbook from his pocket, Marty approached them.

"This is some place." The man held out a clipboard with the invoice on it.

"It is." Marty looked at it, then used the board to help him write out a check. "Thanks for being so efficient."

"No problem." The man took the check, gave Marty a copy of the invoice, and left.

Marty made sure the door closed behind the man, then took the stairs two at a time. He knew where he had asked his clothing to be taken. As Marty made his way to the master suite, he spotted the boxes he'd marked 'bedroom' and then stopped short.

There were piles of clothes on the floor and a guitar was resting against the wall by a dresser.

The smile fell from Marty's lips.

~

Kelsie paddled the raft to the side of the pool and set his glass down. He, then, closed his eyes and absorbed the sun's warmth like a lizard on a rock.

"Dude?"

Kelsie moaned and didn't want to move. "Go away."

"I got dibs on the master suite."

"No. You don't." Kelsie dipped his hand into the warm water. "Move your shit out of it."

He held up his middle finger towards Marty.

"Fine. I'll do it myself."

"Yo!" Kelsie grew annoyed. "I got here first. Fuck off."

Marty threw up his hands. "Why you? Huh? Why the hell would Benjy give you anything?"

"I could say the same thing, ya dumbass." Kelsie's raft floated closer to Marty. "Don't touch my guitar."

"This place has nine bedrooms. Pick one!"

"I did. Leave me alone." Kelsie peeked at him. He saw Marty storm into the house. "Don't touch my shit!" Knowing he would, Kelsie grumbled and slid off the raft and onto the patio. He stood up and entered the home.

He caught up to Marty. "Don't do it."

Marty bounded up the stairs.

10

Kelsie raced after him and they sprinted to the master suite.

Arriving together, they got stuck in the doorway and battled to push into the room first.

They were struggling so much, they both landed on the carpeting on their knees.

"Ow." Marty rubbed his legs.

Kelsie lay on his back and took off his sunglasses. "Stop being a putz." He peeked up and spotted boxes on the floor in a row. "What's that?"

"My stuff." Marty looked at his elbow with concern.

"Well, take your stuff someplace else."

"Hang on." Marty sat up on the white carpet. "What gives you the right? I don't remember anyone saying you had priority."

"God, you're an ass!" Kelsie got to his feet and stood near the boxes. Each one had a label of the contents. Not only the list of the clothing items, but the number of items. "Dude? You own twenty pairs of briefs?"

Marty stormed over and moved between Kelsie and his boxes. "It's better than wearing the same pair over and over."

"I usually don't wear any." Kelsie tried to open a box. "Come on. Let me see how an anal retentive douche packs."

"Don't touch my clothing."

Kelsie hopped on the bed with a bounce, and stretched out over the silky white fabric.

"Are you damp from the pool? What are you doing?"

"God! You're annoying. You're worse than my mother."

Marty made a noise of irritation and left the room.

"Take your twenty panties with you!" Kelsie called after him.

~

Marty was fuming.

When that attorney said he and this guy were splitting the house and bank balance, he had no idea he'd be taking a backseat. He was the one out of the two of them that had any brains.

Benjy would think this was funny.

Marty sat down on a bed in a guestroom and thought about his friend.

'Dahhhling!' Benjy wearing his baggy lounging pants, ones with wild colorful print on them, would hold up his martini glass. *'Just live! Live and laugh. Honey, if you can't laugh...'*

Marty's mouth curled into a smile. Benjy Lloyd was a character. And that was an understatement.

The sixty-year-old man would host elaborate parties, decorate the backyard and pool with fairy lights and pillar candles and create a spread of food and drinks to rival any five-star hotel.

Marty shook his head, and went on the hunt to find another bedroom he liked.

~

Kelsie watched Marty removing the boxes from the master bedroom. He rolled to his side, his head propped up on his palm, and didn't smirk or make a comment to sound superior to Marty.

'You may not have everything you want, Kel, but you have you. Never forget.'

Kelsie thought about Benjy, his laughter, which sounded like a cross between a witch's cackle and a hound-dog's yip. It was fun to make Benjy laugh simply to hear it.

Benjy, in his outlandish outfits, mismatching patterns and colors, baggy cotton pants and Hawaiian shirts, barefoot, wearing wigs, hats, and turbans, plastic bangles and shells...

THE ODD COUPLE

'Youth is wasted on the young. Don't quote me. It may be Oscar Wilde, you know.'

"Hey...Marty," Kelsie said when he returned for another box. "You want this room?"

"Nah." Marty hoisted up the last box and left.

Kelsie climbed off the bed and followed him, seeing where he was going to sleep. Marty had selected a bedroom with a view from the back of the house overlooking the pool and valley.

As Marty unpacked, carefully placing his clothing in drawers, Kelsie reclined on an upholstered lounge chair, one with dark, lion-claw feet and matching pink tasseled pillows. He looked down at his bathing suit and thought about changing, but, since he was lonely, he wanted to hang out with Marty.

As Marty emptied a box, he folded the cardboard and set it by the door.

"He was something else, wasn't he?"

Marty turned to look at him.

"Benjy."

"Yes. He was." Marty opened a second box and began hanging up the clothing in a closet.

"He told me he liked my poetry." Kelsie smiled as he thought about it.

"Knowing Benjy, he probably did."

Kelsie watched as Marty unpacked the second box, folding it with the first once it was empty.

"He told me he'd help me record a demo tape." Kelsie stared into space. "We never did."

Marty glanced over at him, then set a smaller box on a chair and opened it, taking toiletries into the bathroom.

"What'd he promise you?" Kelsie asked.

Marty appeared to be busy in the bathroom. He didn't answer.

13

~

Marty set his toothbrush into a holder, and opened the medicine cabinet. A few odds and ends were left for guests.

After he filled it with his own items, he folded the smaller box and set it with the others. He glanced at Kelsie, who was on his back on the lounge chair, staring at the ceiling.

"He didn't promise me anything."

Kelsie perked up and looked at him.

Marty shrugged. "I never asked for anything."

Kelsie sat up and patted the lounge beside him.

Since they were going to be living together, Marty joined him.

"He was a hoot." Kelsie smiled, as if remembering something.

"I adored him." Marty brushed lint off his slacks. "I remember him wearing these orange baggy lounge pants. They had Orange County prison patterns on them."

"I gave him those." Kelsie chuckled. "I found them at a thrift store."

Marty laughed. "He used to drink orange martinis when he wore them. He said he liked to match."

"Fucking Benjy." Kelsie shook his head. "Did he ever tell you about his first boyfriend?" Kelsie stood up and struck a pose, one hand on his hip and the other holding an imaginary cocktail. "Dahhling! I was so in love!"

Marty covered his mouth to stop the laughter.

Kelsie continued to impersonate Benjy. "We loved and loved and loved!" He batted his eyelashes. "Then? Nothing. No sex. Well, I had no idea why he'd lost interest in my bottom."

Marty chuckled at Kelsie's over-the-top impression, then again, maybe not so exaggerated.

Pretending to sip the cocktail, Kelsie continued, "…I thought he was cheating on poor moi!" Kelsie held up the imaginary drink. "Then! I find *The British Bottom Boy* magazine in his underwear drawer!" Kelsie's expression of pure Benjy-reaction followed. He blew up his cheeks, rolled his eyes, and tossed back his hair, which was absurd, since Benjy was bald, unless he wore a wig, which he did, often.

Marty shook his head in amusement.

"Bye-bye-Brit-Bottom-Boy!" Kelsie waved and then sat beside him. "I peed myself when he told me that one."

"He had a colorful past." Marty stared at his shoes, which were polished to a high sheen.

"Fuck, I miss him already." Kelsie shook his head. "I'm going to get dressed."

"Okay." Marty watched him leave and then thought about Benjy. "Damn. I miss you too."

Chapter 2

Kelsie showered in the enormous marble and brass stall/tub. He took a white towel, one with gold trim and an embroidered 'BLL' monogram. He rubbed it over his hair and then caught his reflection in the mirror over the sink basin.

He remembered Benjy making fun of his beard, his scruff.

Kelsie stepped out of the tub and continued drying himself, missing his good friend a lot more than he imagined he ever would.

He dressed in jeans and a T-shirt, then paused for a moment to look at the collection of clothing Benjy had left in his one of many closets.

It was a rainbow of fabrics and prints, much like Benjy's life; colorful and diverse.

Kelsie touched the soft cotton of one of Benjy's many lounging pants. It was printed with cats on it.

He chuckled.

'If you ever come here and I have eleven felines slinking around, shoot me!'

"Not one cat, Benjy." Kelsie moved the hanger lovingly. He didn't think he could clear out Benjy's things. It just wasn't right. He shut the closet door and headed down the stairs.

The older couple who ran the kitchen were busy chopping, sautéing, and baking.

THE ODD COUPLE

He had seen them at every party Benjy had hosted. Sigmund and Helga. How could he forget those names?

Benjy adored them for their loyalty and culinary skills, but, he still teased them.

'Oh, Helga-dahhhling! I would have married you if Sig hadn't!'

Then, Benjy would make kissing noises at the older woman until she shooed him away playfully.

Kelsie left them alone, seeing his margarita mess had been tidied up. He walked to the end of one of the long hallways and peered into a room, leaning on the doorway.

This was one of Benjy's favorite rooms. His 'man-cave'.

Pinball machines, air hockey, a large screen TV, a music system with surround-sound, and a jukebox. Kelsie stared at the pinball machine, remembering Benjy playing it...while Kelsie fucked him.

Howling with pleasure, Benjy kept slapping the metal ball with the paddles as Kelsie rammed his cock up Benjy's ass.

'My two favorite pastimes!' Benjy gasped. *'Pin-balls and man-balls!'*

Hearing someone behind him, Kelsie turned to look. Marty was there, as if he'd been searching for him.

~

Marty stuffed his hands into his trouser pockets. "Hey."

"Hey." Kelsie moved out of the doorway.

Marty peered into the room. "God, I love this space."

"Look at the porcelain signs." Kelsie gestured to the walls. Highly polished street signs, one that read 'Glory Hole' another said, 'Mother-lode'. Each sign was from an actual location, and not a reproduction.

Marty stood in front of a pinball machine, one that had women in feather boas and bodices. "He used to say this one was his drag-queen phase." He loaded the balls and shot one into the bumpers.

"I haven't found his stash of wigs and dresses yet." Kelsie watched him play.

"Oh, they're here, somewhere." Marty shook the machine and it tilted, stopping the game. "Huh. He used to get away with that."

"He got away with a lot." Kelsie smiled.

"I don't want to change a thing." Marty walked to the jukebox and scanned the selections.

"Me neither. No way."

"Good. I'm glad you said that." Marty pushed the buttons for a single. *What a Wonderful World* sung by Louis Armstrong, played.

Kelsie took a chair, one shaped like a palm cupping your bottom, pink inside, white molded plastic outside. He swiveled side to side.

Marty inspected the walls, which were covered in road and advertising signs. "Ya ever ask yourself, why us?"

"Yes. Since the reading of the will." Kelsie spun around in the hand, raising his feet off the floor. "Did you know he was doing this?"

"No." Marty turned to face him. "I had no idea. I would have tried to talk him out of it."

"He sucked at relationships." Kelsie sat cross-legged on the chair.

"Not really." Marty smiled. "He had hundreds."

"Ha!" Kelsie scrambled to his feet, striking a pose again. "Dahhhling! We were so in love!" Once more he held up one hand as if holding a cocktail and flipped back his hair.

Marty touched his mouth in amusement.

"All he wanted was to be inside me...day, night, day, night." Kelsie pranced around the room. "Then he stays out all night. With the boys...he says..."

Marty tried not to laugh.

"I changed the locks and put his manly work-boots outside!" Kelsie sniffed loudly and held up the invisible cocktail. "Then, he marries a mousy-thing. Says he got her preggo..."

Marty glanced at the jukebox as the song ended.

"What does he do?" Kelsie narrowed his eyes the way Benjy used to do. "Two! Three! Four in the morning! At my door. Suck my cock, he says. I miss your ass, he says!"

"And what did you do, Benjy?" Marty loved the impressions.

"Dahhhling! I sucked his cock and gave him my ass! Two full years after he married his pregnant mouse!"

"Ooh, fuck." Marty dabbed at his eyes. "God, that's right. Poor Benjy."

Kelsie shook off the impersonation. "Meh. He liked it. Benjy wouldn't do anything he didn't like." He leaned over the jukebox and had a look.

Marty's smile fell. "Maybe. But, he really wanted to find that prince."

Kelsie stared at him for a moment, then opened a cabinet under the TV screen. "Well, I found his gay porn stash."

"I don't watch it."

Kelsie flopped down in front of the cabinet and sorted through DVDs.

Marty was about to leave the room and check on dinner, when Kelsie said, "That guy wanted Benjy back."

"Huh?" Marty paused at the doorway. "What guy?"

G. A. HAUSER

"The one that knocked up the woman and married her."
Kelsie glanced at him, an erotic gay movie in his hand. "He said
he'd get a divorce and live with Benjy."

"And?"

"Benjy told him to go fly a kite." Kelsie stacked the DVDs on
the floor beside him. "He even sent him a kite. He really did. On
it he had printed, 'fuck you', in red letters."

Marty smiled. "That's Benjy."

Kelsie slid a DVD into the player and held the remote,
pointing it at the screen.

A video of men inside a fake jail appeared on the enormous
flat-screen, and three tattooed gods were taking turns fucking a
muscular bald man with low hanging balls.

Marty paused to watch.

"Damn." Kelsie looked back at him. "He was kinky as hell."

"That's kinky?" Marty gestured to the film.

Kelsie showed him a DVD. "Guy fucking a horse."

"Augh!" Marty held his hand up. "No."

"Bleck." Kelsie tossed the DVD behind him. "Dude. Some
things have got to go."

"You might be right."

"It's gonna take us years to get through all his stuff." Kelsie
kept looking over the selection. "Gag!"

"No." Marty backed up. "Better you than me. I'll check on
dinner."

"With Hans and Fritz?" Kelsie smirked.

It was then Marty remembered Benjy saying that about
Sigmund and Helga. "Oh, God. Don't say that in front of them."

"I bet Benjy did." Kelsie smirked, still looking through
DVDs. "Oh, ew!" He grimaced and held one up. "Penis up-the-
urethra plugs!"

Marty covered his crotch. "Later." He headed to the kitchen.

~

20

THE ODD COUPLE

Kelsie shivered at some of the raunchy DVDs. He may be curious, but you can't 'un-see' some of this stuff. "Brrr. Benjy, you naught boy." He made two piles; keep and *no-way*!

He noticed several videos that didn't have mass-produced labels, some that were just blank faces with hand-written notes, like; Sam's asshole, or Johnny's slit.

"Okay, Benjy, these I have to see before I toss." He made a third pile. "But, I'm gonna be high first."

~

Marty kept his smile as he headed to the kitchen. The aroma was tantalizing. Since he'd been to several soirees before, Marty knew how good the food could be.

He spotted the dining room table with two place settings and a floral centerpiece. Helga brought in a basket of freshly baked bread.

"Are you serving dinner?" he asked her.

"Soon. Would you care for a cocktail?"

"Not yet. Thanks." He watched her retreat into the working kitchen.

Since there was already water on the table, Marty picked up one of the stemware glasses and sipped it, then stared out of the picture window at the view.

He had never thought of Benjy as a sexual partner. They were close, as close as he had ever been with another person, without sex.

There were many late nights he and Benjy had spent together, discussing films, especially foreign films, mostly French...or Italian...

When that topic had exhausted, Benjy would remove books from his shelves. '*You must read Ayn Rand, dahhling. If for nothing else, for sport.*'

Marty smiled to himself. He had read every recommendation, and seen every subtitled film that Benjy had mentioned. If not for the 'sport' he did it so they could discuss it.

No one stimulated his mind like Benjy did.

~

Kelsie leaned back on his hands as he watched one of the bootleg videos. "Oh, fuck no." He winced as men had their penis pierced without anything numbing them.

"Aaak!" He shut it off, ejected it, and tossed it on the throw-away pile. "Dude." Kelsie shook his head and placed another into the DVD port. A close up of a tongue in an ass, obviously done with a home video camera, was next.

"If you did a sex tape of us..." He thought about it. No. That wasn't Benjy's style. Benjy had enough men willing to perform, surrounding him that he didn't need to sneak.

"Yeck." He removed another one and tossed it on the pile.

"Sir?"

Kelsie looked over his shoulder.

Helga was there. "Dinner is served."

"Okay." He shut off the TV and took the pile of rejected DVDs with him, following the older woman who wore a black outfit down the hall. "What are we having?"

"Roast duck with pears and a vegetable medley."

"Duck?" He was used to burgers, fries, and subs. As he drew closer to the dining room, he made quacking noises.

Marty perked up when he entered the room.

"Quack. Quack, quack..." he muttered, still making the noise as he looked for a place to dump the stack he was holding. "Must find trash."

Sigmund glanced at him, then opened a cabinet and reached out his hands.

"Um." Kelsie shook his head. "Dude, you don't want to touch these while you're cooking." He threw them out and then stood at the sink to wash his hands. "Duck?"

"It tastes like chicken."

At Sigmund's joke, Kelsie roared with laughter. "Oh, Benjy trained you well."

"He did, sir."

"Tastes like chicken." Kelsie dried his hands and peered at the orange-colored bird as Helga sliced the meat. "Duck." He shrugged.

"Would you like a cocktail?" Sigmund asked.

"Why, yes, Sig. I would."

"Anything in particular?"

"Why don't you make me Benjy's favorite so I can toast him?"

"Very good."

Kelsie returned to the dining room and made a silly face at Marty. "The head of the table? Man, what's with you? Are you exclusively a top or what?" He pulled out a chair and sat down at the second place setting.

"You have the master bedroom. Give me a break."

"Fine." Kelsie picked up a roll. "Duck."

"I know."

"No. I mean. Duck!" He threw a piece of bread at Marty's head.

It bounced off Marty's forehead and landed on his china plate. "You're an asshole."

Kelsie tore open the roll and buttered it. Taking a bite, he said as he chewed, "Speaking of assholes. Benj had a homemade DVD called Sam's asshole. Was a tongue licking a hairy hole."

Marty expressed his distaste and, using two fingers, dropped the piece of bread that Kelsie threw, onto Kelsie's plate.

Kelsie popped it into his mouth. "Anal-retentive?"

He got a dirty look.

"Virgin?" Kelsie sipped the water from his glass.

All he got was a roll of the eyes in reply.

Sigmund, a stout-bald man with blue eyes, brought him a martini mixer, pouring it into a glass over an olive.

"Thanks." Kelsie picked it up and sipped it. "Shaken, not stirred."

Plates with appetizers were set down; tapenade and fresh salads.

Kelsie used his fork to smash the tapenade onto his roll.

"Where did you learn table manners?" Marty gaped at him as if he had eaten a turd.

"Duck." He threw more bread at him.

"I can't believe I have to live with you...I can't believe it." Marty moaned and rubbed his face.

"Believe it." Kelsie took a helping of the salad. With his cheeks full he stared at Marty, who was eating like a dainty princess. "I know you're hot for me."

"In your dreams." Marty avoided his gaze.

"How old did you say you are?" Kelsie took another roll.

"Why?"

"I just wanted to see if you're the oldest virgin I know."

"Can we have a little peace while we eat?"

"I don't know. Can we?" Kelsie looked over his shoulder into the kitchen briefly and asked, "Twenty-eight?"

"What?" As if insulted, Marty narrowed his eyes at him. "I'm twenty-five."

"Yup. The oldest virgin."

"I'm not a virgin." Marty was actually cutting his lettuce before eating it, making it bite-sized bits.

Kelsie shoved a whole romaine leaf into his mouth and let the dressing drip down his chin. "Look. Cum."

"Stop."

"Lick it."

"Will you quit it?"

"It's fun turning you on." He licked his own chin.

"You're repulsive."

"Is it in my beard?"

"Gross. Shave."

"Shave? No. I like my manly beard." He rubbed the scruff with his palm.

"You look like an idiot."

Sigmund topped up their beverages, taking empty plates.

"Thanks, Sig." Kelsie used the napkin on his face, getting the dressing off.

"You're welcome."

Kelsie waited until he left the room. "So, you don't drink?"

"I do. Just not every day."

"Do you smoke?"

"No." Marty sipped the water from his glass.

"Not even weed?"

"Oh, my God." Marty moaned and sat back. "Is this how every meal is going to be?"

"What? Duck?" Then, Kelsie remembered and threw more bread at him.

"Cut it out!" He batted the chunk out of his hair.

"Cut it out!" Kelsie mimicked.

A platter was displayed next to him.

Sigmund held it while Helga offered to serve.

Kelsie stared at the carved bird. "What do you recommend?"

He was given a slice of the breast and a leg.

Kelsie stared at it skeptically. He waited for Marty to be served and then watched him eat it.

Marty chewed and then glanced at him.

"You're not spitting it out." Kelsie tried a piece. He frowned. "No, it doesn't taste like chicken." He spat it out. "Gamey."

"You didn't just do that."
"Yo! Sig! Ya got pizza in there?"
Marty closed his eyes and moaned.

THE ODD COUPLE

Chapter 3

After dinner, Marty took a soak in the bathtub of his private suite. As he relaxed he thought about his job as a bank teller and wondered if he needed it any longer.

Both he and Kelsie had been given a massive trust fund, with individual payouts per month; much more than he could hope to spend.

As he thought about giving notice, of not having a structured life, he grew a little nervous.

The door to his bathroom opened and startled him.

Kelsie entered, carrying his guitar. He sat on a padded stool beside the tub and strummed it.

"What are you doing?" Marty covered his crotch under the water.

"Serenading you." Kelsie hit a few chords, then sang, "The wonders of a bath...where a hard-on makes a splash...masturbation creates waves...and duck tastes like shit."

"That doesn't rhyme."

"I know." Kelsie played his guitar, closing his eyes.

"Why are you in here?"

"I get lonely."

"Why didn't I lock the door?"

"*You* get lonely." Kelsie stopped playing, stood, and set the guitar down, leaning it against the wall by the door. "Dahhhling!" Kelsie went into his Benjy routine, "You're going to shrivel up in that bath!" He reached towards the faucets and turned on the hot water.

27

"Stop. Okay?" Marty sat up and went to turn it off.

Kelsie began to battle, blocking Marty's attempt at shutting off the running tap.

"It's too hot!" Marty sat up and made another attempt at stopping the boiling water. It became too warm to tolerate so he stood up, covering his groin.

"There we go!" Kelsie gave his body a sweeping glance. "Meh. So-so."

"Jesus!" Marty climbed out of the tub, splashing water everywhere as he did, picking up a towel.

Kelsie shut off the water, then allowed it to drain. He sat on the stool and gazed at Marty. "I'm horny."

"That's not my problem." Marty wrapped the bath-sheet around him and left the bathroom. He faced the dresser and dropped the towel, putting on clean briefs.

Behind him, Kelsie sang while playing his guitar, "He cupped his balls in the shower stall…we suspect he's a grower, not a show-er."

Marty picked up the shirt he had worn before his bath and put it on, exasperated. "I was just winding down to get ready for bed."

"Bed?" Kelsie looked around. "It's not late."

"I have to work tomorrow." Marty held the tail of the shirt over his crotch.

"Work? Are you insane? We have four grand a month to spend, and this place is already factored in." Kelsie raised his guitar higher and sang, "He wants to work, what a jerk, can't deal with wealth…" Kelsie stopped strumming and asked, "What rhymes with wealth?"

"You're an idiot."

Kelsie sang, "Can't deal with wealth, you're an idiot." He put on a thinking face. "No. That doesn't work."

THE ODD COUPLE

Marty closed his eyes and made a noise of frustration. He dropped to sit on the foot of his bed and covered his face.

~

Kelsie leaned his guitar on the wall by the door. Then he sat down beside Marty, putting his arm around him. "Where do you work, dude?"

"A bank." Marty inhaled deeply and rested his hands on his knees.

"Dude!" Kelsie recoiled. "That's just nasty."

"I don't own it!"

"Bad. Corporate crime." Kelsie held his fingers like a cross warding off vampires.

Marty flopped to his back on the bed with a bounce. "Go away."

"A bank? For real?" Kelsie glanced at the bulge in Marty's briefs.

"For real. It's where I met Benjy."

"No!" Kelsie laughed. "Benjy entered a bank?"

Marty gave him an irritated stare. "Yes. Often. He used to wait for me to be available so I could help him."

"Available?"

"I was a teller. I am a teller." Marty rubbed his face. "I don't know what I am at the moment."

"Rich. Dude." Kelsie used two fingers to hold Marty's shirt, and peek under the tail to see his treasure trail and belly button. He liked what he saw.

~

"Maybe I should take time off to decide. I mean, what will I do all day if I don't work?" Marty waited for the sarcastic comment, and didn't get one. He raised his head up from the bed to look at Kelsie. "What are you doing?"

"I'd fuck that."

29

Marty swatted Kelsie's hand away and tugged the shirt lower over his pelvis. "Are you listening to anything I say?"

"You're a teller and I'm a listener." Kelsie took another peek under Marty's shirt. "Get it?"

"Why are you in my room?" Marty moved back on the bed to make space between them.

"I'm horny!"

"What's that got to do with me?" Marty rolled off the bed and looked at the digital clock on the night table. "Go watch gay porn and jerk-off."

"You suck." Kelsie scooted off the bed. "No. You don't suck. That's worse."

"Hey! I'm having an existential crisis here!"

Kelsie picked up his guitar and sang, "Some men kill to get my dick...how did I end up with a cold prick?"

"Out!" Marty pointed.

"My techniques would make you scream...bet your cum tastes like sour cream."

Marty shoved him into the hall and shut the door.

Kelsie obviously lingered outside the room. "We live together, you angry shit!" he sang loudly, "there's no reason to have a snit!"

Marty could hear Kelsie grumble and walk away.

He sighed heavily and scuffed his feet on the short pile beige carpet. He opened a painted-white end table, one with scrolling gold trim and scalloped edges. Inside was an envelope. He sat on the bed and removed the paperwork, once more reading the details of the contract which dictated the terms of his living arrangements.

Yup. I'm stuck.

He stared into space, knowing, if he gave up his job, he had no other option but to stay here.

"Benjy?" he said, looking up at the ceiling molding and light fixtures, "Are you kidding me?"

~

Slunk low in one of the beanbag chairs, Kelsie exposed his cock from his jeans and then made sure the tissue box and lotion were within reach. He pointed the remote at the large flat-screen TV and watched porn.

A fantastic hunk, with blue eyes and chiseled good looks was getting his big cock sucked by two fabulous young men.

Kelsie set the remote control down and used the lotion on his palm, then pulled on his cock as he enjoyed the act. Close-ups of wet lips on a glistening dick made his mouth water.

A tip of a tongue ran under the head of that big dick and Kelsie felt a surge of climax lust.

He increased the speed of his hand, huffing as the sensation grew to a peak.

"Hey. Can I talk to you?"

"Now?" He held his erection and peeked behind his back. "Whoa!"

Kelsie squeezed the base of his cock and paused the frame on the TV. "No way am I as big as that guy. Christ, two mouths on it and he could fit three." He could see Marty holding up his hand, trying to block the sight of his cock. "Dude? Are you even gay?"

"Yes, I'm gay!"

Kelsie looked at his own dick. "How could you not like it? It's perfect." He ran his palm over it.

"I'll come back."

"No. Watch me. It's hot."

"No."

"Come on, Marty!" He was losing his erection. "Goddamn it." He let go of his cock and started the video again. "What do you want?"

"Can you tuck that in?"

"Do you know how many guys would pay to see this?" He gestured to his cock and balls.

"I'll come back."

Kelsie struggled to stand up from the sinkhole which was the beanbag chair. He stood and met Marty's green eyes as he pushed his soft dick into his jeans. "There. What?"

"Are you going to wash your hands?" Marty kept his distance.

Kelsie glanced at the TV screen; a big dick getting tongue action. He inhaled for calm and then lunged for Marty.

~

"Gross!" Marty was grabbed and Kelsie ran his fingers all over his face and hair. "Yeck! I just took a bath!"

Kelsie tackled him to the floor and straddled over Marty's hips. He folded his arms and glared at him. "Talk!"

"I can't now." Marty winced and wiped at his cheeks.

"I'm gonna jerk off on you," Kelsie warned, reaching into his pants.

"No!" Marty held up his hands. "Don't. I'll talk. Get off."

Kelsie slid to the carpet and waited.

Marty sat up and expressed his disgust, touching his face and hair.

"Well?"

"I forgot what I wanted to say." Marty stood and shivered. "I have to splash my face." He left the room and jogged to the nearest bathroom. He turned on the light and washed his face and hands, then inspected his hair. He let out a loud grunt of irritation and closed his eyes.

~

"You're driving me crazy, and not in a good way!" Kelsie yelled. He stared at the HD screen and then shut off the DVD, muttering profanity. He stood near the jukebox and selected a song. '*Somewhere Over the Rainbow*' played in the surround sound.

"Some joke, Benjy. Some joke." He glanced at the hallway.

~

Back in his own room, Marty brushed his teeth and got ready for bed. He set his phone-alarm so he could wake up for work tomorrow and since it was Saturday, he had a late start and shorter hours. He relieved himself and flushed the toilet, then rinsed his hands and stared at his reflection in the mirror. He checked his teeth, touched his hair, and then shut the light.

Marty moved around the darkened room to the bed and pulled the blanket down, crawling under, exhausted and looking forward to sleep.

"Hello."

Marty grabbed his chest and jumped out of his skin, seeing Kelsie in his bed. "I locked the door!"

"I found a key!" he answered with the same inflection.

Marty moaned and dropped to his back on the bed. "I'm in hell."

"Do you have any idea how scary this house is at night?" Kelsie shivered.

"You wanted the big room." Marty gave him his back and tugged at the blanket.

"Why are you wearing clothes?"

"It's not clothes. It's PJs. Get out of my bed."

"I'm not going back there. It's haunted."

"It's not haunted. Who on earth is haunting it? Benjy?"

"Dahhling! Did I tell you about my luvah?"

Marty sighed.

"We were so in love! We loved and loved and loved!" Kelsie moaned in ecstasy. "He couldn't get enough! He wanted to move in!"

Marty felt Kelsie trying to spoon him and elbowed him to back off.

"Then? The want-want began...Benj, can I have a gold Patek-Phillipe! A diamond tiara! A firm Benz!"

Marty groaned louder and rolled to his back.

"And...he had to go..." Kelsie made a 'tsch, tsch' sound.

"A firm Benz?" Marty peeked over at him.

"I got a firm Benz for you." Kelsie hugged him and pushed his hard dick against him.

"I have to get up for work!"

"Ouch. No need to scream." Kelsie released him.

"Back up!" Marty used his feet to keep shoving Kelsie to the opposite side of the bed.

"Dude!" Kelsie popped off and hit the floor. "Ow."

"Go away." Marty crushed the pillow under his head.

"Don't blame me if you get nailed by an incubus."

"Bye."

The door finally closed and Marty sighed and tried to fall asleep.

~

In a pair of Benjy's brightly colored bottoms, Kelsie walked the long, lonely hall to the master bedroom. With the servants gone it felt creepy as hell.

"Dude." Kelsie shook his head. "Why him, huh? He's a cold-fish." He entered the large white room and left the door slightly ajar. Unlike his housemate, he wanted someone to climb into bed with him.

Kelsie turned on one of the bathroom lights and closed the door partway, letting the glow of the light illuminate the strange room. Yes, it was his first night here...first night here without Benjy.

He climbed under the blankets and pulled them over his head, hiding from the goblins.

Chapter 4

Saturday morning, dressed in a business suit and tie, Marty made his way to the lower floor. He checked his cell-phone, not seeing any missed messages, and pocketed it, then followed the scent of coffee to the kitchen.

"Good morning, Marty." Helga immediately filled a mug with coffee. "Cream and sugar?"

"Cream, yes. Thank you."

"I'll bring it to you."

"Okay." Marty wasn't used to this kind of service. He backed out of the kitchen and noticed several newspapers and freshly squeezed juice already on the table.

The weather was mild for June and sunny, and the sky was brilliant blue and cloudless.

He took a seat at the head of the table as a cup of coffee and a tiny creamer pitcher, were set before him.

"Thanks." He poured cream into the cup.

"I can make you eggs, any style, pancakes, waffles..."

"Um." Marty looked at Helga. "Eggs?"

"Certainly. How would you like them?"

"Over easy."

She smiled and returned to the kitchen. Marty sipped the coffee and had a look at the LA Times.

~

Kelsie squeezed his morning boner. He felt it tenting the cotton fabric of the loungewear, and then grumbled and rolled to his side. The sunshine was trying to motivate him.

He squinted at the brightness and covered his head with a pillow.

~

"Mm." Marty dunked his homemade sourdough bread into the runny yolk. Crunchy hash-browns and bacon accompanied his eggs. "Mm...mmm...mm, mm, mmm!" He wiped his mouth with his cloth napkin. "Perfect!" He chewed on the thick, smoky bacon.

As he munched the excellent food, he brushed off his hands and kept reading the news, this time, the business section.

Helga poured more coffee into his cup.

"Thank you. It's fantastic."

She smiled modestly. "It's just eggs, Marty."

"Made to perfection." He poured cream into his coffee.

"When will you be home?"

"Three-ish. I'm off tomorrow and Monday."

She nodded and retreated into the kitchen.

Marty finished every morsel on his plate and checked the time. He gulped the juice, drank his strong coffee, and then wiped his mouth and hands. He stood from the table, and Helga met him at the threshold, handing him a brown bag.

"Lunch?" he asked in delight.

"Yes." She grinned.

"Wow."

"Have a wonderful day."

"I will. You too." He peeked into the bag as he headed to the front door, seeing the same crusty sourdough bread made into a sandwich. "Mmm!"

~

Kelsie heard noises from below his room. As he stared into space, the sound of a car starting and driving off made him check the time. "No. You're not leaving me here all alone." He sighed and wondered why Marty needed to work. It made as much sense as it did for him to sit on a street corner in downtown LA and play his guitar for handouts.

Kelsie burrowed under the blankets and fell back asleep.

~

Marty parked in his usual spot at a pay-lot. He left his car and straightened his tie as he approached the bank.

Entering it, he locked the door behind him, seeing the armed security guard, as well as his manager, Roy, already there. Marty was about to bring his lunch to the employee lounge when Roy spotted him.

The young man, one whom previously barely acknowledged he existed, nearly hurdled over a low divider to get to him.

Marty inhaled in surprise and held up his lunch bag for protection.

"Marty!"

"Yes?"

"Come to my office."

"My…my lunch." He pointed to it.

"Don't worry. Come."

Marty was waved to follow as if it were urgent.

"Come, come, come." The chair was pulled out for him. "Sit."

Marty did, the small brown bag on his lap.

Roy took a seat behind the desk. "You look snazzy."

"Huh?" Marty touched his tie.

"How long have you been working here, Marty?"

"Three years, four months, and two days."

Roy made a noise of surprise and then straightened his features. "Well, it's about time we promoted you to assistant manager."

A smile came to his face, then Marty thought about it. "Why?"

"A loyal employee? Never short on his till?"

The imaginary light bulb lit over Marty's head. "Ohhh…" He got it. The money.

"We should have promoted you months ago. Your work here is outstanding."

"Roy?"

"I've been instructed to give you VIP parking…"

"Um. Roy?"

"You'll have that office. Right there." Roy pointed.

"Let me guess. I'm now the client with the biggest bank balance."

"No…" Roy shook his head in mock shock. "We're just delighted—"

"Dude?" Marty held up his hand. "I get it." He stood up, clutching the lunch bag.

"The head office instructed me to—"

"I was conflicted. I was." Marty ran his fingers over his tie. "Thanks for helping me make a decision."

Roy's mouth hung open on his next comment.

"I mean it. Thanks." Marty shook Roy's hand and then made sure he had the few personal items he had left behind. He dropped his security pass and keys on the teller window counter. He had a last look around, and was let out of the bank by the guard.

~

Kelsie finally pried himself out of bed. He showered, trimmed his facial hair, and dressed in shorts and a T-shirt. He made his way down the flight of stairs and into the dining room by riding the wooden banister to the ground floor.

A place setting was on the table, as well as a few newspapers. He was about to take a seat when he looked outside the wall of glass.

"Would you like coffee, Kelsie?" Helga asked.

"Yes. Out there?" He pointed.

THE ODD COUPLE

"Certainly."

Kelsie rolled back the sliding glass door and walked in his bare feet to a lounge chair by the pool. He cast his shadow over the man seated on the foot.

Marty, wearing his suit and tie, polished shoes and a wristwatch, munched on a sandwich.

Kelsie dragged a second lounge chair closer, and also sat on the foot, staring at Marty.

Helga brought out a small pot of coffee, setting it with cream and sugar, on a table. "What would you like to eat?"

He asked Marty, "What are you eating?"

"Duck." Marty chewed and swallowed. "Sliced duck, with cranberry sauce, and I think some kind of relish dressing." He looked at it. "Oh, and lettuce."

Kelsie wrinkled his nose. "No."

"I can make you eggs, or perhaps—"

"Eggs. Yes, please. Scrambled, with bacon?"

"Right away." Helga returned to the kitchen.

"Duck? For breakfast?" Kelsie held his mug and sipped the coffee. "Oh, that's damn good java."

"Lunch." Marty licked his finger. "I already had breakfast."

"I'm confused." Kelsie shivered at how smooth the coffee tasted. "Damn. I need this in an IV."

Marty used a paper napkin on his hands and opened a small brown bag, removing grapes.

"Where did you get that?"

"Helga made it." He popped one into his mouth.

"Why the bag?"

"It was to-go."

"Still confused." Kelsie topped up his coffee.

Once he finished chewing, Marty said, "I was given a promotion."

"That's nice."

39

"So, I quit."

Kelsie coughed on his sip and cleared his throat. "Dude. You need help." He pointed to his own head. "In here."

Marty set the grapes down on his lap. "It wasn't because of me or my performance. It was because of Benjy's bank balance."

"So?"

"Nope." Marty put what was left of his lunch on a glass table. "That's wrong on so many levels."

"Okay..." Kelsie humored him.

"There're five employees who have been there twice as long as I have."

"Okay..." Kelsie nodded.

"All of them women."

Kelsie paid attention.

"I get a big number in a savings account and boom. Promoted."

"Dude." Kelsie shook his head. "I hear ya."

"Now, I want to change banks."

Shrugging, Kelsie said, "Change banks."

"Yeah?"

"Yeah."

"Thanks."

"Nothing overseas."

Marty rolled his eyes.

"No high risk Ruskie banks."

"Shut up."

Kelsie glanced over his shoulder as Helga brought him a plate of food. He set his cup aside and she moved a small glass-topped table closer and served him.

"Oh, man, that looks good." Kelsie smiled at Helga. "I love you."

"I love you too." She laughed and took the trash from Marty's lunch.

Kelsie chewed on a crunchy bacon slice.

"I'm going to gain so much weight living here." Marty sighed.

"We could work it off." Kelsie moaned as he stuffed the hash-browns into his face. "Why are you wearing a tie?"

"Oh." Marty loosened it and slid if off.

"Go put on a bathing suit."

"It's too cold."

"The pool's heated. Go." Kelsie scooped the scrambled eggs onto the sourdough bread, added the bacon and made a sandwich, devouring it.

"I hate being bossed around." Marty lay back on the lounge chair.

"Two tops, no bottoms." He swallowed the food in his mouth. "Thanks, Benjy." He caught Marty giving him the stink-eye. "What?"

"Is sex all you can think about?"

"Dahhling!" Kelsie held up his coffee mug. "I was so in love! We loved and loved and loved!" He batted his eyelashes. "Then? Nothing. No sex." Kelsie exaggerated his sorrow with the back of one hand pressed to his forehead.

Marty chuckled.

"Get married, he whined!" Kelsie acted out the drama the way Benjy had described the tale. "He wanted to adopt babies! So many babies!" He sat up and ate more of his food. "And...he had to go." He caught Marty smiling at him and winked.

~

Hanging his suit up in the closet, Marty kept his smile. *All right, he's growing on me.*

The true comedy was in the fact that Kelsie's impersonations were spot on. He couldn't count the number of times Benjy had whined about loves, loves-lost, and new ones replacing the old ones.

Chuckling out loud, Marty made sure his suit was clean before hanging it on the rack in his closet. Taking off the shirt, he folded it for laundering.

For once, he didn't have to press his own clothing.

In his briefs and socks, Marty opened a drawer looking for a casual outfit.

He heard noise and turned to see Kelsie had leapt onto his bed with a bounce.

"Do you ever knock?" Marty put on a pair of jeans.

"Kiss me."

"No." He faced his back towards Kelsie and zipped up.

"Why not?"

"You're not my type." Marty removed a shirt from a drawer and put it on.

"I thought we were going to swim."

"It's too cold." Marty faced him, tucking in his shirt.

"What's your type?"

Marty fussed with his shirt.

"Alive?" Kelsie laughed. "A pulse?"

"God! Just when I think you're tolerable." He checked his phone. No one had sent him a message, so he placed it back down.

"Hey."

"What?" Marty looked up at him.

"Duck." He threw a pillow.

"Jerk." Marty picked it up off the floor.

"It's a throw pillow. You do realize they call it that for a reason."

"You're a moron." He tossed the pillow back on the bed and left with his laptop.

~

THE ODD COUPLE

Kelsie relaxed on Marty's bed thinking about Marty quitting work, and the reason for it. It was sort of noble, him leaving for being promoted. Or, maybe stupid.

Kelsie held the throw pillow under his head and stared at the dresser. He got to his feet and had a look at some of the items that had been placed in a straight line on it.

Prized personal possessions?

A carved wooden box containing tie-bars and cufflinks, a ceramic skunk, and a framed photo. Kelsie picked up the small frame to inspect. It was a picture of Marty with Benjy. They were holding up cocktail glasses and laughing.

Kelsie set the photo down and stared in the direction Marty had taken.

~

Seated in a sunroom with his laptop, Marty looked up banks online and studied their interest rates, their customer satisfaction reviews, and their lending practices.

He typed his thoughts on a document file and then sat back to consider his actions.

Nah.

He deleted the file and shut down the laptop.

Something hit the back of his head.

Marty touched his hair and turned to look.

"Duck?" Kelsie was in the doorway of the room.

Marty narrowed his eyes at him and stood up. On the floor was a blue ball made out of sponge.

Kelsie retrieved it and tossed it up and down. "Wanna watch me juggle?"

"No." Marty tucked his laptop under his arm and made a move to walk by him.

"I'm bored."

"Why is that my problem?" Marty headed to his room. Behind him, Kelsie used his back to bounce the soft ball and catch it.

Tolerating it, Marty entered his room and set his laptop on a nightstand, then he spun around and caught the ball that was thrown at him. He squeezed it in his palm because it was soft and felt nice. "I'm not good without a routine."

"Okay." Kelsie shrugged.

"I've been working since I had a part-time job in middle-school."

"Okay..." Kelsie held out his hand for the ball.

"What am I supposed to do all day?" Marty tossed him the ball.

Kelsie held it up, as if it was a torch and he was the Statue of Liberty. "I decree every day shall be Martin Hayes Day."

Marty caught the devilish gleam in Kelsie's eye. "You're persistent. I'll give you that."

"You ain't seen nothin' yet. It's only been one day."

"Two. If you count today."

"I don't count it." Kelsie bounced the ball off of the ceiling.

Marty made a move to leave the room.

Kelsie tucked the ball into his shorts, giving him a huge bulge. "Where're you goin'?" He pushed his hips out and squeezed it.

"You're insane." Marty headed for the staircase.

"Give it a squeeze. Come on."

While holding the railing, Marty turned towards Kelsie and shook his head at his antics.

Chapter 5

Okay. I'm really bored.

Kelsie knelt on the floor in the master bedroom closet, opening plastic bins, which were neatly stacked. He set the top aside and removed the brown paper from the interior. He'd found some of Benjy's wigs.

"Ha! Awesome." A plethora of colors, styles and lengths were packed in individual zipper bags, with hairnets protecting them. Kelsie noticed one platinum blonde wig and placed it on his lap, unzipping the pouch. A shimmering cascade of hair slid out.

He removed the netting, and the ball of paper from inside it, and put it on. The long locks flowed down his shoulders.

Kneeling up higher, Kelsie tried to get a peek at himself in the full-length mirror behind the door. Seeing himself with a scruffy beard and a blonde wig made him crack up.

"I love you, Benjy." He kept it on and moved the bin aside and chose another. Inside this one, were shoes; once more, every color of the rainbow, every style; from stilettos to platform boots, suede to snakeskin.

"Dahhling!" Kelsie picked up a red suede boot to admire.

~

Marty finished reading an ebook on his tablet. Yawning, stretching his back, he knew he had to find something meaningful to do with his life if he did quit work.

45

He stared at the jukebox and the pinball machines, the metal and porcelain road signs on the walls, and the giant flat-screen TV.

Motivating himself, he stood and set the e-reader aside, then headed to look for Kelsie. He'd been left alone for hours and wondered what his housemate was up to.

Wandering the halls, hearing Helga and Sigmund in the kitchen, as well as landscapers trimming the shrubs outside, Marty peeked into the large bedroom suite.

The walk-in closet door was open and light was shining out of it. He drew closer, hearing rustling.

When Marty stood at the doorway he saw Kelsie was wearing a red leather outfit with high spiked black boots and a blonde wig.

Since he heard Marty enter, he spun around and smirked. "Dahhhling!"

"You found his stash." Marty noticed several open plastic bins.

Kelsie tried to saunter closer, and ended up wobbling on the high-heels, turning on his ankle and grabbing the hanging clothing for balance. "His feet were bigger than mine."

"Nope. You can't pull it off the way he could."

Kelsie kept closing the gap between them, and fell, the heels tripping him up. Marty caught him and tried to get him upright.

"How did he walk in these things?"

The wig became askew and made Kelsie appear even more ridiculous.

"You look like the bearded lady, not a drag queen."

Once he helped Kelsie gain his balance, Marty stared at the big bulge in the leather pants. He pointed it out. "Blue ball?"

"Yes. You're killing me."

"No! I mean…" Marty exaggerated his frustration.

Kelsie squeezed it playfully. "Honk, honk." He peered down at himself. "I like having a big bulge."

Marty ignored him and sat down next to the tub with the wigs in it.

Kelsie removed the foam ball and sniffed it.

"Ugh." Marty spied him do it and shivered. He turned his attention to the wigs.

Kelsie sat down beside him and tugged off the boots. He straightened his wig and had a look at what Marty was doing. "You'd look hot with long hair."

"No. I wouldn't."

"Yes. You would." Kelsie dug through the plastic zippered bags and produced one, holding it out.

"I'm not trying on a wig."

"But, dahhhling! For Benjy!"

Marty stared at him, seeing his wicked smirk. He kept tapping Marty with the plastic bag. "Fine. I'm that bored." He took the wig out of the sturdy bag.

~

Kelsie brushed the blonde hair out of his mouth, blowing it off his lips as it stuck. He waited as Marty tried on the long brown-haired wig. He placed it on his head and fussed with the length, which was to his chest in front.

"You're a rock-star."

Marty attempted to see beyond him to the mirror.

Kelsie tackled him and pinned him to the floor, pulling on Marty's jeans and stuffing the sponge ball into his pants.

"Dude!" Marty tried to fend him off, but Kelsie managed to get the foam ball into his jeans.

"I like it!" He squeezed the soft ball from over Marty's zipper flap. "Nice."

Marty stopped battling and stared at him. "Can I ask you something?"

Kelsie kept squeezing the sponge ball, getting excited. "Yes. Whatever you want."

"Why did Benjy choose us?"

"Oh." Kelsie stopped what he was doing and sighed. "I guess he liked us." He brushed the blonde hair out of his eyes.

Marty removed the soft ball from his pants and rolled it on the carpet.

Kelsie picked it up to sniff.

Marty took off the brown wig and carefully returned it to its bag. "He liked a lot of people."

Kelsie tapped the blue ball on his chin as he thought about it. "Well, he may have felt sorry for me. I was a poor street urchin."

Marty put the boots back into the shoe bin. "I wasn't."

"How close were you to him?" Kelsie removed the wig and tucked it away.

"Close. We used to discuss everything from politics to books for hours." Marty sealed the bin, pushing the plastic lid down until it snapped into place.

"And the sex?"

Marty slid the bin under the hanging clothing. "Huh? Sex?"

"Yeah. How was the sex?"

"We didn't have sex."

Kelsie blinked and stared at him. "Wait. What?"

"We didn't mess around." Marty stood and straightened his shirt. "Did you?"

"Yes! I pounded his ass all over this place." Kelsie got to his feet and took off the leather outfit, folding it and placing it in another bin.

"You did?"

Kelsie dropped the leather pants to his ankles and stepped out of them, standing naked as he did. "Yup."

~

Marty gave that information some thought. "Wow. That's harsh. I guess I wasn't his type."

"You're my type." Kelsie used his thumbs to rip the blue spongy ball open and stuck it on his dick, like a clown's nose. Then, he put his hands on his hips and swung it side to side, hitting his pelvis.

Mesmerized for a second at the hypnotic act, Marty shook himself out of it and left the walk-in closet.

The ball hit him in the back of the head.

"Duck."

He narrowed his eyes at Kelsie and walked down the hallway to his own room.

~

Kelsie put his shorts and shirt back on and picked up the ball, tossing it up and catching it in his palm. *Why didn't Benjy have sex with you...hmm.*

It didn't take long to figure out. And it wasn't because Marty wasn't attractive. He jogged down the hallway and found Marty in his room, standing at the sliding glass doors which opened to a tiny deck and a view of the valley. "You're an exclusive bottom."

"Huh?" Marty seemed distracted.

"You only bottom."

"Sex again?" Marty opened the sliding doors.

Kelsie stood beside him, staring at Marty's profile. "What exactly turns you off about me?"

"One thing."

"What's that?"

"Your personality."

"Ouch! Dude." Kelsie winced and rubbed his upper arms. "That's harsh." Then, he thought about it. "But, you like my body?"

"Aaarugh!"

"I'm twenty-eight! I want sex!"

"I'm not stopping you!" Marty yelled back.

Kelsie gave up. He left Marty's room and returned to his. He picked up his phone and scrolled through his contact list.

~

Marty stood on the small balcony, leaning his arms on the rails as the strong wind blew his hair around. *Benjy couldn't have been matchmaking. Me and Kelsie are polar opposites.*

He rested his chin on his hands. "You're not funny, Mr Lloyd."

~

"So, you're busy?" Kelsie asked his friend Pablo, as he walked towards the game room.

"Yeah. I'm working."

"I keep forgetting it's…wait. It's Saturday."

"I work weekends."

"Oh."

"I've got to go. See ya."

Kelsie stared at his phone and then entered his favorite room. He left his phone on a table by a pinball machine and dropped to his knees, looking into the TV table cabinet for something to jerk-off to.

~

Marty wandered around the big house, inspecting all nine bedrooms. Each had been decorated in a different color-scheme and style. The master bedroom; white, his bedroom; beige, another, pale blue, yet another, mauve…and on and on.

Each had an adjoining bathroom, also color coordinated. Marty opened closets and drawers, but other than sheets and towels, nothing was left in them.

He remembered his e-reader and headed to the game room, since it was by far, the most interesting room in the house. And, it was where most of Benjy's parties ended up.

THE ODD COUPLE

As he drew closer, he could hear the sound of grunting and cheesy music. He stood at the doorway, and there was Kelsie, lying nearly prone on a beanbag chair, jerking off to another gay porn video.

Before he did an about-face and left Kelsie to himself, he watched the big screen; a man was jerking off on another man's face, while the same man was getting fucked from behind.

Kelsie gasped and Marty watched the cum spatter Kelsie's low abdomen. He stayed put while Kelsie milked his dick, squeezing out drops.

A tingle from chills rushed down Marty's spine. He bit his lip, touched himself lightly, and decided to retrieve his e-reader later.

~

Kelsie turned towards the doorway when he felt someone watching. He caught Marty walking off. "You can join me, ya know!" Kelsie called after him, but didn't get an answer. He wiped up the mess with tissues and stopped the video. "This sucks."

After he rolled off the soft beanbag chair, Kelsie washed up, straightened the room and looked for Marty. It felt like they were stranded on an island with only each other for company.

He spotted Marty outside by the pool, lounging under an umbrella, reading a paperback.

Kelsie sat on the same chair, and stared at him.

Marty appeared to struggle to keep reading, peeking at him.

The glass sliding door opened, and Helga brought out a tray of snacks and lemonade.

"Thanks," Kelsie said to her.

"My pleasure."

He waited as she set up her treats on a small table, and then returned to the house. Kelsie took a handful of mixed nuts and munched them, staring at Marty as he did.

~

Since Kelsie had joined him, Marty had reread the same line over and over. He shifted his legs so Kelsie had more room, then finally gave up and met his gaze. "You realize we're going to lose our minds here."

Kelsie tossed a peanut up and caught it in his mouth, chewing.

"I mean...the two of us, unemployed, sad, lonely—"

"Sad and lonely? Speak for yourself." Kelsie took another handful of nuts.

Marty gestured to the empty pool area. "Where are all your friends?"

"I have them. They're busy." Kelsie held up a nut and said, "Open wide."

"I know where your hands have been."

"I washed them." He took aim.

"I don't want a peanut."

"It's a cashew."

Marty held out his hand.

"Uh-uh."

Marty knew he'd be pestered until he complied, so he humored him.

Kelsie tossed the nut into his mouth.

Marty chewed the cashew. "Can you pour me a glass of lemonade?" He set the book he was reading on the patio.

Kelsie picked up the pitcher and poured the liquid into a tumbler glass filled with ice. He handed it to Marty.

Marty took it, sipped it, and then put it on the patio beside his novel. "Maybe I shouldn't quit work."

Kelsie smirked at him, then inched up Marty's legs to be nose to nose with him. "You do realize I can be your sex toy."

"In your dreams." Marty tried not to smile. He'd never been pursued. But, he had a feeling, giving in to a guy like Kelsie was a bad idea. He only wished Benjy were alive so he could get the 411 on the guy.

"Skinny dip with me." Kelsie ran his hands down Marty's arms to his wrists.

"It's too cold out. The wind."

"It's warm in the pool. It's heated." Kelsie tugged on him.

"I've never skinny-dipped in my life." Marty glanced at the patio doors.

"Come on. Christ. How on earth did you and Benjy become friends?" Kelsie stood at the foot of his chair and started to undress.

As Kelsie dropped his clothing, Marty shifted on the padded chair.

Once naked, Kelsie reached out his hand.

"I'm not comfortable being naked."

"In briefs then." Kelsie headed to a plastic storage box that was near the side of the house. He opened it and dug through it.

Marty stared at Kelsie's ass, his slender figure and unabashed sense of freedom.

Florescent 'noodles' were tossed into the pool, as well as rubber balls, whimsical animal-shaped inflatable rings, and even a plastic shark.

Kelsie held a hot pink foam noodle between his legs and walked towards him. He pretended the noodle was his dick and slapped it on Marty's legs. "Come on. Don't be chicken. It's just me."

He was tempted. "Are there towels?"

"Of course there are." Kelsie tapped the end of the noodle on Marty's cheek.

Marty batted it away and exhaled loudly. He looked at the house, then stood, removing his socks.

~

"Yes!" Kelsie did a cannonball into the pool, splashing water over the ledge. He popped up and slicked back his hair. The water was very warm, like bathwater. Using two noodles to float on top of, Kelsie watched Marty as he took paranoid glances behind him at the house, finally making his way to the pool.

Wearing dark briefs, Marty covered his bulge and used the stairs at the shallow end of the pool.

Kelsie liked Marty's body, and was attracted to him.

"It is warm." Marty kept moving into the deep end.

"Why would I lie?" Kelsie swam closer. "Wanna wrestle?"

"No." Marty held a raft under his arms and floated around. He hadn't even gotten his hair wet.

Kelsie picked up a beach-ball from the surface. He used his palms to pop it up and down into the air. "Wanna volley?"

"Nah." Marty rested his head on his arms and paddled gently.

Kelsie held the ball in his hand and began bouncing it off Marty's head.

"Quit it."

He did not.

Marty moaned and held up his hand to deflect it. "I mean it."

Kelsie batted the ball onto the patio then jumped on Marty's back, dunking him under the water.

Marty used the bottom to brace himself and torpedoed back up.

Kelsie hung onto him, his arms around Marty's neck, his cock brushing Marty's bottom.

"Get off."

"No." Kelsie tried to keep Marty off balance.

"I mean it!" Marty pulled at Kelsie's arms. "This is why I can't swim with you!"

Kelsie reached under the water with his left hand while holding Marty in a headlock, and tugged Marty's briefs down his hips.

THE ODD COUPLE

"Dude!" Marty nudged Kelsie off his back and dunked him, pushing him down to the pool bottom.

Kelsie held his breath and spun around while under the water. He got a grip on Marty's briefs in both hands, and jerked them down to his knees.

He heard Marty shriek in panic, as he reached for them.

Kelsie toppled him over and slipped the briefs off Marty's legs, then surfaced and spun them around like a lasso.

Marty gave him a look of exasperation. "Give them to me."

"No." Kelsie played keep-away.

Marty made a few attempts at them as Kelsie dodged him. "You suck!"

Kelsie spun the wet briefs and tossed them as far as he could.

They got stuck on a shrub by the fence and hung in a dark wet blob. He sank under the water and swam towards Marty's legs, seeing his hand cupped over his soft dick, as well as a nice trimmed pubic bush and treasure trail. He sank to his knees on the bottom and held Marty's hips as he surfaced for a breath.

Marty stumbled back in the water, and reached for something to stop himself from falling.

Kelsie wrapped both arms around Marty's thighs and pressed his mouth against Marty's crotch. As he did, he blew bubbles against Marty's dick.

Marty stopped struggling.

~

While he stared at his underwear sagging from a rosebush, Marty tried not to panic about someone seeing him naked. A sensation of tickling rushed over his cock and balls.

He blinked and grew aroused. As his brain deciphered the source of the tickling, he made a decision if he liked it or not. Kelsie picked him up off his feet and sat him on the edge of the pool.

As Marty reached back for the cement to stop from falling, Kelsie surfaced between his legs and sank his cock into his mouth.

Marty nearly fell over at the surprise attack. He gasped and spread his toes as chills rushed over his wet skin.

"Mmm!" Kelsie sucked him to the base.

Gasping to catch his breath, Marty began to sink to his elbows on the warm patio as the sucking made him insane.

~

Kelsie held the base of Marty's slender, straight, circumcised dick and used his tongue to draw squiggled lines on it.

He heard Marty gasp and peeked up at him. Marty jumped from fright and Kelsie spotted a landscaper, making his way to the potted shrubs which surrounded them.

As they both registered the stranger in their midst, Marty pushed Kelsie away and scrambled to his feet, cupping his crotch and grabbing the clothing he had folded on the foot of the lounge chair.

Kelsie caught his breath as Marty's tight bottom vanished as he escaped into the house. He watched the landscaper, and didn't even get eye contact. If this man had worked for Benjy for any length of time, nothing he would see would surprise him.

He dragged a raft closer, brought it under his arms and floated on the surface.

The man spotted the wet briefs, picked them up, set them on a chair, and didn't blink as he trimmed the dead flowers.

"Ha." Kelsie chuckled.

~

Marty stood under the shower's spray in his private bathroom. His hand slick with soap, he jerked off and kept his eyes closed. Though the deed unnerved him, it also got him excited.

THE ODD COUPLE

He came, squeezing his cock and shivering at the potency of the climax. Once he relieved himself of the desire, he let the hot water pelt him, wondering if Kelsie had been this sexually aggressive with Benjy.

Chapter 6

After hiding in his bedroom all afternoon, Marty grew hungry. He had reorganized the bathroom cabinet, placing his items in groups; hair products, skin products, shaving products…

He was losing his mind.

He poked his head out of his room and made his way down to the kitchen. The one thing he wished Benjy had included in this house was a home-gym. There was nothing here to work out with, except the pool and it wasn't big enough for laps.

Tiptoeing his way down the stairs, Marty had a peek over the rail to the foyer. He caught the scent of food and his stomach grumbled.

He made his way across the marble floor, his socks not making a sound.

"Dahhhling!"

Marty grabbed his chest in fright and turned around.

Kelsie had a red feather boa around his neck and wobbled on high heels.

Marty gave him a look of irritation and stopped sneaking. Seeing the dining room table set with two place settings, he took his usual seat and sipped the ice water.

The boa was dragged over his head.

He batted it away as Kelsie grabbed the back of a chair to stop from toppling over. "How does anyone walk in high heels?"

"Why are you wearing them? You look absurd."

"The clothing in that closet is sick." Kelsie plopped his bottom onto a chair and pushed the ends of the boa over his shoulder. "Why did you disappear?"

"I had things to do."

Helga brought over a tray of appetizers, stuffed mushroom caps. "Do either of you want a drink?"

"Yes, please." Kelsie picked up a mushroom cap and crammed it into his mouth.

"Wine? Beer? A cocktail?"

As he chewed, Kelsie said, "Decisions, decisions."

"I'll have white wine. Any kind of white." Marty used tongs to take two mushroom caps to his plate. "Maybe not Chardonnay. Um. No. Make it red. Anything but Merlot."

Kelsie groaned and rolled his eyes, popping another stuffed-cap into his mouth.

"Something sort of sweet." Marty set the tongs on the platter. "Um, maybe Riesling? Or, what about blush? Rose?"

"Oh, my God!" Kelsie pretended to pound his head on the table.

"Or, maybe not wine. I mean, I don't know what you have. I should just drink—"

Kelsie bopped Marty on the head with the tail of the boa. "Just get him a sweet cocktail."

"Very good." Helga covered her smile and left.

"Don't make decisions for me." Marty used his fork to cut a mushroom cap in half, eating it.

"Why not? You seem to suck at them." Kelsie continued to eat off the platter.

"I don't." He blew a red feather off the table as it landed soundlessly.

"These are awesome." He licked his fingers.

Marty stared at Kelsie for a moment. "There's no gym equipment in this place."

"Benjy said he was allergic to exercise." He took the last mushroom cap and ate it, his cheeks bulging.

"What do you think about converting one of the first floor bedrooms into a workout room?"

"Mm. Sure." He nodded, wiping his hands on the boa.

Marty narrowed his eyes at him. "Don't do that. Use a napkin."

Kelsie shook out the cloth napkin ceremoniously, flapping it at him.

"Why! Why did he stick us together like this?" Marty moaned and rubbed his eyes.

While Marty was distracted, Kelsie took a mushroom cap off of Marty's plate and ate it.

Marty peered at him through his fingers.

"Mm." Kelsie smiled as he chewed. "Your dick tastes better."

After taking a paranoid look into the kitchen, Marty ate the tiny bite of food left on his plate and crossed his legs, thinking about getting sucked and then jerking off in the shower.

"We can fuck to burn calories." Kelsie kept tossing the feathery boa behind him as it slid onto the table.

Red feathers continued to float and Marty puffed them away before they landed on his plate.

"Huh? Tonight?" Kelsie made a gesture, pushing his finger through a gap he'd made with his thumb and index finger. "Bam. Bam...oh, yeah..."

"Stop."

Helga returned, setting two reddish colored cocktails on the table, each with their rims coated in sugar and a ripe strawberry.

"Nom, nom!" Kelsie tossed the boa behind his shoulder and picked it up, sucking down the contents.

She took the appetizer plates, silverware, and platter, and left them alone.

Marty watched Kelsie finish the strawberry drink, then Kelsie held his forehead in pain.

"Brain-freeze." He winced.

"You're an idiot." Marty ate the strawberry, leaving the tiny green stem, then tasted the drink. It was a strawberry daiquiri, and as rich as a dessert.

While still recuperating from his frozen brain, Kelsie held up the glass. "More please?"

Marty felt something on his lip and when he touched it with his tongue, he immediately began to try and get it out of his mouth. He held up a wet feather. "Can you take that thing off?" He shook it from his hand and batted away the floating feathers.

Kelsie looked at him, and unraveled it from his neck, stuffing it on the vacant chair beside him. He removed his strawberry and held it up for Marty, tempting him.

"I'm good."

Kelsie made the noise of an airplane and tried to land the strawberry in Marty's mouth.

"Dude!" Marty sat back and became exasperated.

Kelsie ate the strawberry, then spit out the leafy stem.

"Seriously." Marty wasn't joking. "I don't want to eat with you. You're making me sick to my stomach."

"And, you're no fun. Like zero." Kelsie held up his hand, making an 'O' with his fingers.

Marty pressed his palms together to beg. He stared at the ceiling. "Why, Benjy? Why?"

"At least I gave him climaxes." Kelsie sipped the last drop from the daiquiri glass.

Helga brought them two plates, holding them with white towels. "Very hot." She set one in front of each and Marty inhaled the aroma.

"What is it?" Kelsie asked.

"Gnocchi with pork belly, in a sherry sauce and arugula."

"I have no idea what you just said, but it smells great." Kelsie dug in and moaned in pleasure.

"Thanks." Marty smiled.

"You're welcome." She took Kelsie's glass and brought him a fresh daiquiri.

"I love you!" Kelsie gobbled the food.

"I love you too!"

"Sig does all the prep, Helga, the heavy lifting." Kelsie slurped his drink.

"I need to work out. Holy shit this food is good."

"Pork belly." Kelsie rubbed his own stomach, bloating it out and oinking.

"Please stop." Marty stuck his fork tines into a gnocchi. "I don't want to hear animal noises from the food I'm eating. It's really unsettling."

"Whatever." Kelsie focused on his food. "Oink."

It was quiet for the rest of the meal.

~

After dinner, Kelsie brought the boa and shoes to the master bedroom closet. He returned the items to their boxes, and then picked up his phone to see if anyone had sent him a text message. Nope.

He left his phone behind and decided to hit the game room to either watch a movie or play pinball.

Trotting down the stairs, he slid on his socks across the marble floor, and then danced his way, playing air-guitar, to the game room.

Marty was already in it, curled up on the chair shaped like a palm, holding an e-reader.

"Oh." Kelsie's plans for noise got derailed.

Marty exhaled deeply and kept reading.

Before he asked Marty to relocate, Kelsie took a look at the selection of comic books and novels on a built-in bookshelf along one wall. Just as he was going to ask for a recommendation, he heard a loud splash coming from the direction of the pool.

Marty looked up and then at him. "What was that?"

Kelsie headed to the kitchen, wondering if Helga and Sigmund may still be here. They usually left after dinner.

With Marty following him, Kelsie was able to see out of the glass sliding doors. To his astonishment, people were gathered around the pool, swimming and drinking.

"What the?" Marty stopped short. "Did you invite friends over?"

"No." He and Marty stood at the glass, staring out of it. "This is weird."

"Who are they?" Marty asked.

"Should we ask?"

"Hang on. It's our house, right?" Marty seemed to be checking with Kelsie.

"Oh. It is." Kelsie inspected each individual. "Yup. I recognize some of them. Benjy's entourage?"

"Shit. What are we supposed to do?" Marty touched the latch on the slider.

"Um. Do you care if they party?"

"That's a really good question." Marty glanced at him.

"I guess it's what Benjy would want. Right?"

"Did they hop the fence? How did they get in?"

"He never locked the gate. You knew that, right?"

Marty gave him a look that seemed to say he did not know. "I came through the front door. Silly me."

"Stop being a dork." Kelsie ran his hand over his head, then his facial hair, then he stood tall and took a deep breath. "I'm going in."

"Good luck."

"If I don't come back alive, remember how much I loved you." Kelsie flipped open the latch and slid back the glass door. Laughter, shrieks, splashing, and loud music overwhelmed him. He took a last look at Marty, and stepped outside.

~

Of course Marty knew Benjy had wild parties. But, he didn't know he'd be hosting them without giving out an invitation.

He stood at the glass door, watching Kelsie mingle with the crowd of people.

"I give you credit, Mr O'Loughlin." Marty leaned his shoulder on the metal door frame, crossing his arms. He wasn't a fan of chaos and had usually spent time alone with Benjy, enjoying their intellectual chats.

The deep reverberating echo of someone falling into the pool made Marty jump. If it were up to him, he'd ask them to leave.

In the glow of fairy and solar garden landscape lighting, more people appeared, walking like shadow figures out of the darkness.

The last thing Marty wanted was for them to come inside the house. He closed the slider, and latched it. "Nope. Uh-uh."

A water balloon hit the glass.

Marty jumped again, this time, out of his skin. He spotted Kelsie pointing at him.

Marty backed away from the door. "You're locked out, dude. I guess I'll have the last laugh." He made sure it was indeed latched, then drew the vertical blinds over it, and ran his hands over his hair nervously.

~

Kelsie tried to get in on a conversation.

He stood behind the shoulders of two people, both of whom had alcoholic drinks in their hands and he knew they had brought their own.

"…I don't know how she puts up with it."

THE ODD COUPLE

"Neither do I...the nepotism is out of control."

Kelsie glanced at someone splashing someone else from inside the pool. He snapped back into attention. "What are we talking about?"

He was given a look as if he were an irritation.

"Anyway...she gave me a slush pile of scripts to read. Like I have the time?"

"Huh," Kelsie said, still trying to get in on it, "Slush piles. I could read some."

The two people walked off.

"Hey! You do know this is my house and pool, right?" He looked at the sliding glass doors, but Marty had pulled the blinds.

~

Marty hid in the game room, headphones on, his e-reader in his hands, curled up in the 'hand' chair, losing himself in his novel.

Occasionally he'd hear something loud coming from behind the house, and cringe. He peeked up at the wall, staring at a traffic sign, and bent his knees tighter to his chest. If he had any say in the matter, he'd stop strangers from coming here and using the pool.

"Sorry, Benjy, I'm not you."

He shifted the headphone away from his ear to listen. Yup. They were still there.

He cranked up the volume and disappeared into his novel.

Chapter 7

Sunday morning, Marty opened his eyes to bright sunshine. He rolled to his back and recalled the noise continuing well into the morning hours.

After listening, hearing wonderful silence, Marty peeled off the blanket and washed up in the bathroom. He dressed in a clean pair of jeans and a polo shirt, then peeked out of his bedroom door.

Marty slowly made his way down the stairs, holding the smooth wooden banister and keeping his senses alert.

He smelled food and coffee aromas, and knew Sigmund and Helga had arrived.

Marty entered the dining room, and the blinds were open once more. Outside, Sigmund was picking up bottles, trash, and discarded clothing, wearing gloves, and using a reaching-tool grabber.

"Good morning." Helga smiled at him.

"I am so sorry." He gestured to the patio.

She held up a coffee pot. "Coffee?"

"Yes. Thanks." Marty stood at the sliding door, and noticed something. He opened the door, walking to a lounge chair and stood looking down at it.

Kelsie was sleeping, curled in a ball under a pile of towels.

"I'm sorry, Sigmund." Marty picked up a few bottles with his fingertips. "I had no idea."

"Not to worry."

Marty spotted trash floating in the pool and wiped his hands on a towel.

"Dude…" Kelsie moaned. "You locked me out."

"I know."

Kelsie sat up and rubbed at a stain on his shirt. "Damn." He placed his bare feet on the patio.

"Who were they?" Marty asked, watching Sigmund clean up the area quickly, a seasoned vet.

"I have no idea. They blanked me."

"They did?" Marty was very surprised.

"Fucking elitist pigs." Kelsie scratched his jaw through his beard. "Sorry, Sig."

"No problem."

"I'm getting a security lock for the gate." Marty crossed his arms.

"You're not going to get a debate from me." Kelsie managed to get off the chair and staggered to the house.

"Hung-over?" Marty asked.

"No. My back is a mess. You try sleeping on a lounge chair in the freezing cold wind." He entered the house through the slider.

Guilty, Marty watched Sigmund toss the glass and cans into a bin for recycling. "I feel terrible about this. It won't happen again."

Sigmund smiled at him. "You don't have to keep apologizing."

"Yeah. I do." Marty entered the house, seeing Helga had poured his coffee for him. He added cream and carried the cup with him up the stairs. He entered the master bedroom, hearing the shower running. Marty stood outside the door, sipping the coffee.

"Kel?"

"Yeah?" he replied from inside the shower stall.

"I'm sorry. I didn't mean to lock you out."

"Sure ya didn't."

"I didn't want anyone coming inside." He blew on the coffee and then gulped it, since it was so good.

"Didn't you hear me banging?"

"No. I wore headphones and then, went to bed."

The shower stopped and an arm reached out from the steamy doors for a towel.

Marty held his empty cup in his hand. "So, like, no one spoke to you?"

"Nope. No one." Kelsie brushed his hair after he wrapped the towel around his hips.

"And, you didn't know one person?"

"I didn't know anyone." He filled a toothbrush and scrubbed his teeth.

"That's fucked up. I mean, now that Benjy's gone, it's not like we don't have a say in it."

"We do have a say." Kelsie spit out the toothpaste and rinsed his mouth. "Those idiots are not welcome back."

"Good." Marty thought he'd have a fight. He was pleasantly surprised. "Who do we ask to get a lock on the gate?"

"Maybe Sig knows." He spread gel on his face and shaved around his designer stubble.

Marty watched him. Well, Kelsie may be annoying. But, he was cute.

~

Seeing Marty in the mirror, Kelsie rinsed the blade and finished up, splashing his face. "How do we give Sig more cash for the cleanup duty?"

"Huh?" Marty perked up, as if he'd been daydreaming. "I don't know. We could just get cash from the bank ATM."

"That's a good idea." Kelsie put on deodorant and tossed the towel over the rack. He approached Marty. "Let me get dressed."

Marty, holding a white porcelain cup close to his chest, backed up.

"Are you okay?" Kelsie asked him, then rubbed his low back as it ached. "I need a painkiller."

"Sorry. I mean it."

"You should be." Kelsie opened a drawer and put on a pair of shorts. He glanced at Marty, who was still in the same spot. "What's for breakfast?"

"I don't know." He held up the cup. "I only got this far."

Kelsie located a clean T-shirt and put it on. He didn't tuck it in. Once he checked his phone, he headed down the stairs.

With Marty behind him, Kelsie spotted Helga waiting for them. The two of them sat in their usual spots and Helga poured coffee for them.

"Helga," Marty asked, "Who did Benjy use when he needed some DIY stuff done?"

Kelsie stirred milk into his coffee and craved the caffeine.

"Let me get you the name." She returned to the kitchen.

"There's no way Benjy did it himself." Marty held his cup.

"Benjy? No way. He didn't even know how to hammer in a nail." Kelsie finished the coffee, craving more. "Ya know, when you locked me out, I couldn't even get my guitar."

"They would have thanked me."

"No..." Kelsie tried to be patient, since he wanted more coffee and a painkiller. "They would have fallen in love with me and asked me to cut a demo."

"You're delusional."

Helga returned. She handed Marty a business card, then topped up their coffee, and even set a bottle of ibuprofen beside Kelsie. He blinked and stared at her. "Am I nuts? Did I ask you for them?"

"You're not nuts. And if I slept on the patio, I'd need them." She smiled warmly at him.

"I love you." Kelsie shook three tablets into his hand.

"I love you too." She left the coffee pot this time, and vanished into the kitchen.

Kelsie swallowed the pills with orange juice, and then sank in the chair, dying for them to work.

"So, do you want to come with me to buy exercise equipment?" Marty flicked the business card with his fingernails.

Kelsie stared at Marty's hands, the tapping growing annoying.

"I was thinking, maybe a treadmill, or a bike, and maybe free weights, or a universal, or maybe—"

"Dude!" Kelsie snatched the card out of Marty's hand and set it on the table.

"Fine. I'll go by myself and you get the lock done on the fence."

Kelsie rubbed the back of his neck, trying to get the kinks out. "Do what?"

"Come on! Work with me."

"Don't yell. I'm fragile." Kelsie held up his hand. He noticed Marty sit back, so Kelsie looked behind him. Helga had two plates of food.

"French toast. Nice." Marty smiled.

"It smells good." Kelsie waited for Helga to set it down, seeing sausages and a small fruit salad. "That's not your average sliced bread. What is it?"

"Egg bread. Challah. We buy an unsliced loaf so we can make thick pieces."

Marty dipped it in maple syrup. "That's divine."

Kelsie took a big bite and moaned. "You're right. We need a gym."

Helga brought the coffee pot into the kitchen to refill.

"Oh, my God." Marty expressed his pleasure at the food. "Vanilla...what else? Cinnamon?"

"Nutmeg?" Kelsie savored the flavor.

"Almond? Is that anise?"

"Thank you, Benjy!" Kelsie gobbled the food.

~

Marty checked his phone, seeing no one had sent him a text or tried to call. He stuffed it into his pocket, then made sure he had his wallet and keys.

He glanced around his room, then shut off the light and headed towards Kelsie's bedroom. He met Kelsie in the hall.

"Ready?" Marty asked.

"Yes. I'm driving." Kelsie started down the stairs.

"I'm not riding in that shitty dirty car."

"No! You idiot, I'm driving the Bentley."

Marty thought about it, then hurried to catch up with Kelsie. "The Bentley? You're going to drive Benjy's car?"

"I sure as shit aren't going to let you drive it."

Marty watched curiously while Kelsie opened a drawer in the kitchen, one with many keys. "Dude! How do you find all this stuff on your own?"

"I snoop." He cupped the keys and grinned. "Shwah-eet!"

Marty clamored behind him to keep up as Kelsie headed to the front door.

The garage was a separate structure, and could hold five cars.

He used a remote control to raise a single garage door, and there was the car with the personalized plate, 'BENBENT'.

Feeling helpless and a little stupid, Marty gave in and opened the passenger's door, sitting down. "Wow." He touched the dashboard and inhaled the 'new-car' smell.

"Ha!" Kelsie hit the gas as he backed out of the garage, causing Marty to grip the interior and gasp.

"Wooohooo!" Kelsie tapped the garage door remote to close it, then skidded around their parked cars to the main street.

"Slow down!" Marty managed to get his seatbelt on.

"Damn! This is awesome."

"Do you even know where you're going?" Marty held on for dear life.

"No."

"Slow the fuck down!" Marty tried to take his phone out of his pocket to get the address of the sporting goods store.

"Fuck it. Let's hit the beach instead."

"Kelsie! I'm not prepared for the beach! I don't have my sunscreen or towel." He cringed as Kelsie sped down the street. "Stop it! I'm going to be carsick."

Kelsie slowed down and glanced over at him. "Don't throw chunks in a car this nice."

Marty caught his breath and tried to stop feeling panicked.

"Beach."

"No. Drop me off."

"You're my hostage."

"Why, Benjy? Why did you do this to me?"

Kelsie laughed wickedly and kept driving west.

~

Kelsie pulled into a parking spot that someone was vacating. Venice Beach. "Look at that." He gestured to the sand and sea.

"I need Dramamine after that ride."

"And I thought Benjy was the *drama*-queen." Kelsie shut the engine and climbed out of the car. He inhaled the sea air and looked up at the clear blue sky.

He took off his shoes and stuck them near the car tire, then ran towards the sandy beach, feeling the hot, silky grains between his toes.

~

Marty tried to gather his thoughts. He checked his pocket for money and paid for the parking spot. Lesson learned. If he wanted to get an errand done, he couldn't go with Kelsie.

Now he was stuck.

THE ODD COUPLE

He looked for the crazy loon and walked over the pavement, avoiding skaters, joggers, and bathing beauties flexing their muscles.

Kelsie had vanished in the crowd.

Sunday at the beach. It was mobbed.

He held his hand over his eyes, shielding the glare, and searched the sand.

Then, he heard Kelsie calling his name.

Kelsie was wearing just his shorts, waving at him from the water.

Marty walked closer, feeling the dry sand getting into his shoes and socks. He crossed his arms as he watched Kelsie spearing through waves and laughing.

"Come on in!" Kelsie yelled, gesturing for Marty to join him.

Under his breath, Marty said, "What the fuck? Dude, you're insane." He cupped the sides of his mouth with both hands and yelled, "Where's your stuff?"

Kelsie pointed.

Marty scanned the area and there was Kelsie's shirt in a pile. He picked it up, and under the shirt were his wallet, his phone, and the car keys. He held the keys and thought about leaving Kelsie here.

But, seeing him frolic, bouncing around in the surf and sun, Marty didn't have the heart. He sat down beside the little pile of belongings, and stared at the horizon, the buzz of laughter and seagulls in his ears.

~

Kelsie did his best to coax a dud like Marty into the water. He grew weary of trying, and rose and fell over the waves. He then waded out, and stood dripping in front of him.

"Now you're stuck in wet clothing." Marty looked up at him.

"I'll dry off. It's warm out." Kelsie sat beside him, his wet shorts getting coated in the sand.

73

"You're a mess. You're not getting back in the car."

"Dude?" Kelsie wondered if Marty ever let go and had fun. "I'm trying to figure out why Benjy stuck us together as well. You suck."

"I suck?" Marty pointed to himself. "I wanted to get us exercise equipment. You wanted cash from the ATM. Now I'm stuck with you."

"We could order the shit over the computer. We have Benjy's credit and debit cards." He brushed the sand off his hands. "Pick the item, click buy, and have it shipped."

"Oh." Marty stared at the waves. "But."

"Oh, my God!" Kelsie whined. "What now?"

"How do we know what we want to buy?"

"You're pissing me off." Kelsie glared at him. "Are you telling me you never buy online?"

"No. Of course I do. But with stuff we're going to use for a gym, don't you think we should try it out?"

"Try it out? Like run on a treadmill?" Kelsie shook his head. "I'll do it."

Marty took a scoop of the dry sand and allowed it to fall through his fingers, staring at it with a vacant expression.

Kelsie thought about the two of them being stuck together. He then, thought about his dear friend. He missed him. He'd give back everything to have Benjy with him again.

~

Marty got lost in his head as the soft sand blew out of his palm in a stream. He kept chiding himself, knowing with time he and Kelsie would figure it out. It was jarring for Marty to be uprooted from his routine, not working, and now having to coexist with his polar opposite.

He was about to say something to Kelsie when he spotted a tear running from his eye. "Are you okay?"

Since his hands were sandy, Kelsie used his shoulder to try and dab at his eyes. "Let's go."

"Aren't you still wet?"

Kelsie stood and brushed off the sand from his legs.

"Dude? You can't sit in the car like that."

Kelsie picked up his shirt, phone, and wallet. "Where're the keys?"

Marty showed them to him.

Kelsie started heading to the car. On his way, he bought a rainbow-striped beach towel at a drugstore and held it over his shoulder.

Marty had no idea how Kelsie did it. Everything about him was spontaneous and improvised.

Once they were beside the car, Marty knew Kelsie wanted to drive, but, so did he. They both stood on the driver's side. He watched Kelsie rubbing off the sand, then he stepped into his shoes. "Key?"

"I'm driving. Remember the ATM?"

"There's one right there." Kelsie pointed. "In the same place where I bought the towel."

"It's not our bank."

"So?"

"We'll get charged a fee." Marty used the fob to unlock the door.

"So?"

"Dude! I'm not paying to take my own money out of the bank."

"That's right. You're a teller." Kelsie walked to the passenger's side. "How could I forget?"

"What are you going to sit on?"

"The towel." He shook it out and folded it, then dropped it on the seat.

Once Marty sat behind the wheel, he noticed sand still on the backs of Kelsie's calves. "It's a cruel joke."

"You're telling me?" Kelsie slouched low on the leather seat. Kelsie looked at his hand, then wiped at his eyes. "I fucking miss him."

Marty backed out of the parking spot. "Yeah. I do too."

Chapter 8

Kelsie soaked in a warm bath. His back and neck were still aching from sleeping outside on a patio chair. He rested his head on the edge and closed his eyes.

~

Marty clapped his shoes together, getting the sand out of them. He removed his socks and there was sand between his toes. Sighing in exhaustion, Marty walked through the home and up the stairs to his bedroom. He put his socks into the laundry chute, and then washed his hands and feet. Once he felt clean, he put on fresh socks and sat with his laptop and a credit card, searching the internet for good deals on gym equipment.

As he poured over reviews, ignoring the extreme ones and trying to get to the real ones, he managed to order enough to keep himself trim while eating rich food.

And, he had them shipped overnight for free.

Pleased with himself, he carried his laptop with him to show Kelsie what he had decided to buy. He looked into Kelsie's room, seeing his damp shorts on the floor with the shirt he had worn. "Kel?"

He peeked into the bathroom, finding Kelsie relaxing in the tub. "Hey."

Kelsie looked drowsy and raised his head from the edge.

"Can I show you what I bought?"

"Later." Kelsie shut his eyes again.

"Can I at least tell you, so I don't OCD over this shit all day?"

"I'm sure it's fine."

Marty sat on the closed toilet lid. "I bought all the stuff from the same place, since they gave a bundle discount and free shipping. Look." He showed Kelsie his order form.

"Mm." Kelsie didn't even peek.

"Well, they're coming tomorrow, so if they suck we can—"

"Dude?"

Marty shut off the laptop and held it on his legs. He exhaled tiredly. "Are you going to get the lock done on the gate?"

"Yes. I'll call the repairman."

"Okay." Marty stared at Kelsie as he relaxed in the tub. "I put the cash in an envelope in the kitchen with Sigmund's name on it."

"Cool."

He frowned to himself and rubbed at a fingerprint on the computer's surface. "Sorry I locked you out last night."

"Whatever."

Marty stood and left the room, his laptop under his arm. Maybe he shouldn't be so rough on Kelsie. After all, they were both trying to understand why Benjy did what he did, and adjust to a new lifestyle.

He brought the laptop back to his room and picked up his phone. No one had sent him a text, or called.

~

Kelsie peeked. Marty had left the bathroom. He motivated himself and pulled the plug on the bath, draining the water. He hoisted himself out of the tub, and stepped onto the mat, wrapping a towel around him as he dried off. The sand had fallen to the bottom of the bathtub and he was glad to have it out of his crack.

Kelsie tossed the towel over the shower door, then entered his bedroom and stepped over the dirty pile of clothing. He picked up his guitar and sat on the foot of the bed with it on his lap.

THE ODD COUPLE

Strumming it lightly, Kelsie thought about how incredibly rude the people were to him last night and imagined composing a song about them. He ran his fingertips over the strings and then flopped to his back on the bed.

It didn't seem to matter that he was rich. The feeling of loneliness continued.

If he had the choice between money and his dear friend, he would choose Benjy.

He set the guitar on the bed beside him and curled into a ball, feeling deep sorrow growing in him that he couldn't shake.

Benjy validated him.

He listened to him when he spoke, allowed him to play his songs, clapped for him.

Now?

He was stuck with an uptight dude who didn't even want to kiss him.

"Thanks a lot, Benjy."

~

Marty chose which room he wanted the equipment to be in. It was a first floor bedroom facing the back of the house, with large picture windows, containing only a single bed and highboy dresser. He wasn't sure he liked making decisions this big on his own, but it didn't seem as if Kelsie cared.

He made his way to the kitchen and spotted Helga and Sigmund chopping vegetables and kneading dough on the counter.

"Um." Marty tried to get their attention.

"Would you like something to eat?" Helga asked, setting her knife down on a cutting board. "I can make your lunch now."

"Sure...Sigmund?"

"Yes?" He wiped his floury hands on a towel.

"How do I get the mauve bedroom cleared? I'm having exercise equipment placed in it tomorrow."

"I'll take care of it."

"Oh. Cool." He looked for the envelope he'd left, saw it was gone, and didn't ask about it. He watched the couple working as a team and envied them for their relationship.

He left them alone, and stood at the sliding door, staring at the pool which was being cleaned and serviced after the fiasco of last night.

Since Helga was going to make them lunch, Marty trotted back up the staircase and down the hall.

He stood at the open master bedroom doorway and Kelsie was naked, curled in a tight ball on the bed, his guitar beside him.

Just as he was going to leave Kelsie on his own, he heard a soft sob. Marty perked up and waited. Yes, Kelsie was crying.

"Kel?"

As if being upset embarrassed him, Kelsie wiped at his eyes roughly and then he sat up, taking the guitar to his lap.

Marty sat on the bed next to him. "I..." He was going to update Kelsie on the room he'd decided to create into a gym, but he had a feeling Kelsie didn't really care. "Mean people suck."

Kelsie glanced at him, his fingers hovering over the strings. "I suck?"

"No. I'm talking about the people who crashed here to party last night."

Kelsie played chords, not singing, just strumming a melody.

Marty listened to the music, liking it. "So, Benjy was your benefactor?"

"Nope."

"Did he help you financially?"

"Nope."

"Why not?"

Kelsie paused. "I didn't let him."

THE ODD COUPLE

Marty got lost in Kelsie's green eyes for a moment. "Why didn't you let him?"

"He was too nice. No way. He helped me when I was desperate, but I didn't want him to support me."

"But, you benefited once he died."

Kelsie shrugged and played more chords.

"Helga's making lunch." Marty stood, straightening his shirt.

Nodding, Kelsie set the guitar aside.

Marty tried not to stare at his cock. When Kelsie caught him peeking, Marty expected a sarcastic rebuking. It never came.

~

Kelsie found a clean pair of shorts and a cotton shirt in his drawer. He put them on and picked up his phone to check to see if he missed any calls or texts. No one had tried to contact him.

He left the phone on the dresser, and turned to look at Marty. The desire to be loved and accepted by Marty was strong. But, Kelsie knew you couldn't pester your way into someone's heart.

He ran his hand over his hair and left the room. As he descended the stairs and made his way to the kitchen, he remembered the lock on the fence.

Although he could see Helga setting the table in the dining room, Kelsie opened the slider and stepped outside.

The pool was being skimmed, vacuumed, and tested for chlorine levels. Kelsie walked on the soft grass to the side of the house. The gate had been left open.

He inspected the handle. It wasn't damaged.

Just as he was about to return to the house to call a handyman, he noticed something shiny sticking out of the peat moss. He picked it up, brushing it off. It was a padlock. It wasn't rusty or old.

Even though he didn't know if they had a key, it was a way to keep out unwanted guests for free. One thing he agreed with

Marty about was being frugal. Just because you inherited money, didn't mean spending it without a care.

He'd grown up on the street. He wasn't going to go back to them from being stupid or careless.

He hooked the padlock on the gate and shut it with a click.

~

Marty sat at the dining room table, facing the sliding doors.

Helga placed a platter of deli meats, cheeses, spreads, and salads.

A relish dish was presented with pickles, olives, and marinated vegetables.

"Thank you." Marty took two slices of marble rye bread to his plate.

"Enjoy."

Marty piled the thinly sliced meats and cheese on his bread, then spread Russian dressing on it. He chewed a pickle and sliced the sandwich in half, just as the sliding door opened and Kelsie entered.

Kelsie didn't meet Marty's gaze, or smile. He vanished into the half-bathroom, the one closest to the kitchen, and returned, taking a seat.

Marty stared at him, worried.

Kelsie had stopped dancing.

Helga brought a pot of coffee over to them, offering it.

"Yes, please." Kelsie gave her his cup and continued to build a sandwich.

"I'm good," Marty said, his hand over his cup.

Helga retreated into the kitchen.

Kelsie made a thick sandwich of the deli meats, and cheeses, then spread a creamy horseradish dressing on it, along with a handful of alfalfa sprouts.

He picked it up and took a big bite, the bread sliding on the amount of meat inside it.

Marty frowned and stared at his plate.

The silence was painful and awkward.

Seeing Kelsie devour the great food, Marty picked up the half sandwich, eating it.

Kelsie set his down, brushed off his hands and left the table. He returned from the kitchen with a bag of potato chips, dumping them on his plate and adding a few to his sandwich.

Marty thought it was curious since there was potato salad on the table. "Are you mad at me?"

Kelsie shook his head, his cheeks full of food.

"Are you sure?"

Kelsie finished chewing. "I'm mad at Benjy."

"What for?"

"Dying."

Marty set the sandwich on his plate again. "He talked about death with me."

"He tried to pull that shit with me. No way." Kelsie popped a black olive into his mouth.

"He wasn't afraid of it." Marty sipped ice water. "He told me it was just a transition to another place."

"Well, I hope he's happy there because I miss the fuck out of him." Kelsie stopped eating and appeared about to cry.

"I didn't mean to upset you."

Kelsie stared at the table for a minute, then scooted back the chair, and left the room.

"Kel?" Marty called after him.

Helga entered the dining room. "Is the food okay?"

"Yes. Thanks."

She nodded, cleared a few empty cups, and returned to the kitchen.

Marty felt incredibly guilty. He wasn't exactly being nice to Kelsie or acting like a friend. As he battled internally on whether to eat the meal, not wanting to offend Helga and Sigmund, or run to Kelsie to comfort him, Marty ended up getting himself into a state, and had no idea what to do. Then...he had a thought.

~

Kelsie sat in the game room with his guitar.

On a beanbag chair, his eyes closed, he composed a tribute song to his good friend.

"You never locked your door. You cared less that I was poor. With open arms you let me in. When all I knew could be scribed on the head of a pin..." He heard rustling and opened his eyes.

"Dahhling!" Marty wobbled on high heels and had wrapped a pink and yellow boa around his neck.

Kelsie had no clue what to say or do in reaction.

Marty nearly fell over, the heel turning his ankle, and he gripped the doorframe. "I was so in love! We loved and loved and loved!" He batted his eyelashes. "Then? Nothing. No sex." Marty cleared his throat and spit out a floating feather. "I found him having sex with a stripper. He gave me crabs!"

Kelsie shook his head and rested his chin on his guitar. "Ya know the sad part?"

"Me in heels?" Marty stepped out of them, moaning and rubbing his toes.

"No. How many times men broke Benjy's heart."

Marty uncoiled the boa and draped it over the jukebox. He sat on the floor beside Kelsie. "I know. He was unlucky in love."

Kelsie set his guitar aside, crossed his legs, and stared at Marty. "I sort of offered."

"Offered to?"

"To be his boyfriend."

Marty waited for him to continue.

"He told me no. He said I was too young and pretty." Kelsie scratched his jaw. "I think he was afraid I'd hurt him too."

"But, you guys made love?"

"Yeah. We did. Not, like, too many times. A few." Kelsie ran his hand along his shin. "I tried. He kept telling me I had so much more to do before settling down."

"I never imagined me and Benjy as a couple." Marty looked up at the walls, reading the gas and oil signs. "I guess he wasn't into me physically. We didn't touch sexually. I didn't really want to. I loved our quiet talks. He was an intellect."

"I must have been stupid, because we didn't have deep discussions."

"Did he mention my name to you?"

"No. He never did." Kelsie shifted his bottom on the beanbag chair. "Did you know about me?"

"No."

"How long did you know him?"

Marty pulled a second beanbag chair closer and rested his chin and arms on it. "He came to the bank for years. I told you. He waited for me to wait on him. I just thought he was nice."

"And, he asked you out?"

"Not like a date. We had coffee first. Then, he told me to come by anytime. I did."

"I don't remember seeing you at any of his parties."

"I didn't go to any. I made sure I saw him mid-week. He told me he had gatherings. I wasn't into it."

"I feel as though I missed out." Kelsie positioned himself on the beanbag the same way Marty had. They were facing each other, the soft bag under their chest and chins. "Did he think I was stupid?"

"Maybe he thought I was ugly."

"That's not Benjy's style. I know he used to camp it up and play, but he liked people. He saw the good in them."

Marty didn't answer.

"Right?"

Marty let out a low sigh. "He knew some of his 'friends'," he used air-quotes, "were out to get what they could."

"Yeah. He told me that as well. I never asked him for a damn thing."

"Me neither."

"Wait."

"What?"

Kelsie had a thought. "That's why."

"What's why?"

"Maybe that's the reason he had for leaving all his stuff to us."

"Because we didn't ask him for anything?"

"Yes."

"You may be right. I mean, he didn't complain constantly about being used, but I knew he had to have been. Benjy was so damn sweet."

"Think about it." Kelsie sat up on the beanbag. "You know all those guys who *lovvved him, dahhhling*?" Kelsie threw back his head as he said it, "Well? They lost him, didn't they?"

Marty mirrored Kelsie's position, sitting up higher. "Yes. He used to tell me they didn't hurt his feelings, but I knew they did."

Kelsie thought about it. How sweet Benjy was to him. "He didn't deserve to be treated like that."

"He wasn't gullible. He knew. He knew consciously that some of those men were going to hurt him."

"He did. He joked about it to hide his feelings."

"That sucks." Marty ran his hand over his hair. "I wish I could have protected him."

"He wouldn't have appreciated it. Benjy was…well…Benjy." Kelsie shrugged. "I bet if you could ask him now, he'd say he wouldn't change a thing."

Marty frowned. "I'm not sure I agree. I think Benjy craved a real boyfriend. A true heart."

THE ODD COUPLE

"Who doesn't?"

Marty scooted closer. "Do you think he was matchmaking us? I mean, we're so different."

"I did think that when I first heard the reading of the will. But after we sort of clashed, I changed my mind."

Marty's blue eyes were glossy, as if he were either tired or unhappy.

Shrugging, Kelsie said, "We don't have to be partners. We just have to get along well enough to live together."

"That doesn't make sense."

"Sure it does. This is a big house. We don't even have to see each other."

"That's insane."

Kelsie stared at Marty. "Do you hate me?"

"No!"

"But, I irritate you, right?"

Marty went to reply, and then appeared to think about it.

"I'm a little messy? Maybe flighty?"

"I have OCD. I'm the one that's hard to deal with."

"Yeah? OCD?"

"I think so. I mean, organizing my toiletries by body part?"

"Yo…what?" Kelsie cracked up.

The blush immediately hit Marty's cheeks. "Never mind."

"Did you alphabetize them too?" Kelsie started to laugh.

"No." Marty chuckled.

Maybe it was the break they needed to snap out of their somber mood, but Kelsie cracked up and rolled off the beanbag chair.

Marty joined his laughter, dabbing his eyes as he smiled.

Chapter 9

Kelsie played his guitar quietly while Marty read from his e-reader. They may have differences, but the more Kelsie was learning about Marty, the more he realized the amount they had in common.

Kelsie stopped composing music, and set his guitar aside. A thought occurred to him.

Men their age usually had their phones permanently attached to their hands.

Kelsie wasn't interested in being 'connected' constantly, and to his surprise, neither was Marty.

"So…" Kelsie didn't want to disturb Marty's reading, but they had been quiet together for hours.

Marty perked up and set the tablet down. He was curled up in the 'hand-chair'.

"No phone?"

Marty expressed his distaste. "I can't stand my phone."

"Oh?" Kelsie scooted across the floor to sit in front of him.

"If I admit something, will you throw it in my face?"

"You're gay."

Marty rolled his eyes and exhaled.

"Sorry. You were going to make a confession to me?"

"Whatever." Marty held his reader back up.

"Dude. Talk to me. I won't throw it back at you."

After time to consider, Marty met Kelsie's gaze. "No one sends me text messages or calls me."

"Huh." Kelsie bent his knees and wrapped his arms around them.

"I know. I'm a loser."

"No one sends me messages either."

"Really?"

"Yes. And I'm never on the social networks. I fucking hate them."

"Why?" Marty set his reader on the floor and faced him.

Kelsie stared into Mary's blue eyes, losing himself in them for a moment. "Judgment."

"Ahh, yes. Judgment."

"Not only that. It seems as if everyone is either in competition to show how happy they are, or the opposite. It's like a façade of masks. I mean, I can't deal with it. It's a time suck of epic proportions."

Marty nodded in agreement. "I can't recall when I last logged on to the networks. I get depressed easily."

"What about family?" Kelsie slid closer, almost touching Marty's feet.

Marty pouted and avoided eye contact.

"Yeah. Me too."

"Did you tell Benjy this stuff?"

"Yup."

It appeared to give Marty food for thought.

"Maybe he knew better than we did about how we would get along." Kelsie wanted to touch Marty but didn't know if he should.

"The weird thing is, he was a great listener and gave good advice, but when it came to his taste in suitors, he lacked sound judgment."

"Don't we always do when it comes to ourselves?"

Marty finally met his gaze. "Maybe."

Kelsie knelt upright, making an attempt at leaning on Marty's lap, testing the waters. "Have you ever traveled?"

"Do you mean overseas?"

Kelsie rested his forearm on Marty, his chin on his arm. "Anywhere at all?"

Marty didn't shove him off or give him a dirty look. "Um. Not really. I mean, I came to Southern California from Spokane."

"Huh." Kelsie rested his cheek on his forearm. "I'm from Reno."

"Are you in contact with anyone from there?"

"No." He felt Marty touch his hair lightly. Finding comfort in it, Kelsie stayed quiet, wanting Marty to touch him.

"Me neither. I didn't leave after a fight or anything. I just decided to go."

"I fought."

"I'm sorry."

"Why? You didn't do anything." Kelsie relaxed, indeed finding solace.

~

Marty ran his fingers through Kelsie's soft hair. Having Kelsie open up to him about his feelings, sharing, that's what Marty needed. Being an island of pain, of loneliness, sucked.

The contact from Kelsie, him resting on his legs, was warm and comforting.

Marty didn't know if they could be sexual companions, but this kind of affection was welcome. He was starved for it.

And Benjy had provided so much nurturing and warmth, that when he died, Marty felt the void like a black hole.

He liked petting Kelsie's hair.

"Do you have any future aspirations?" Marty asked.

"No."

"Really? Not even cutting a demo recording?"

"Hell, no." Kelsie shifted his arm on Marty and resettled. "That world is so filled with liars, cheats, and greed, I'd get used and abused."

"So, then, nothing to aspire to?"

"No." Kelsie seemed to relax from the light petting. "What about you? Did you want to own your own bank?"

"No. No way." Marty ran his fingers over Kelsie's shoulder and neck. "It was bad enough being a teller. I was lucky I never came up short. My OCD brain would never get over it. I'd freak out and think I was going to go to federal prison."

"Wow. That's rough."

"It's all part of my mind-game. I mean, I do it to myself. I was never threatened. But, the fear alone kept me counting every penny."

"You'd make a lousy bank owner."

"I would. I'd make a lousy everything. I can't manage people. I can't own my own business. Everything scares me."

Kelsie squeezed Marty's leg in comfort.

"Benjy used to tell me he was afraid too." Marty ran his hands down Kelsie's upper back and then into his hair. "That he would be mocked behind his back, or used."

Kelsie raised his head, his expression one of exhaustion. "Yeah. He told me that too. He said he didn't trust anyone anymore."

"He told me the same thing." Marty offered a sad smile.

Kelsie braced himself on both of Marty's knees and went for a kiss.

Since he wasn't expecting it, Marty recoiled and the back of his head hit the chair behind him.

Kelsie blinked and parted his lips to respond verbally, but his expression fell. He stood, picked up his guitar, and left the game room.

Marty held his chest as he absorbed the act, trying to figure out if he felt attracted to Kelsie physically. And if they did mess around, what would happen to them once it failed?

~

Kelsie carried his guitar up the stairs.

On his way, Helga caught up to him. "Dinner will be served in an hour."

"Okay." Kelsie continued to his room. He set his guitar into its case and looked out of the window at the view of the valley and hills. He opened a drawer and removed a tin cigarette box. He stuck a rolled joint into his mouth and lit it with a match. He inhaled the smoke, walked to the window and opened it, blowing the exhale outside.

Knowing how strong the weed was, he took two hits, enough to calm his anxiety, and pinched it out, exhaling the smoke. Kelsie had no idea what to do.

He wanted a lover, a partner, a boyfriend...a husband.

If he dated now?

He'd be dealing with what Benjy had dealt with, money-hungry suitors.

Ironically, his poverty had put men off. Now? His money would bring in idiots and users.

And...

The fact that Marty would not kiss him crushed his ego.

He set the rest of the joint into the small case, and flopped to his back on the bed to calm down from the rejection.

~

"No." Marty realized what he had done. He raced out of the game room and skidded in his socks on the polished marble tile. He grabbed the banister and raced up the stairs, down the hallway to Kelsie's room.

Out of breath, he stopped short, smelled pot, and saw Kelsie lying on his back on the bed.

92

Kelsie raised his head up to see him, then stared at the ceiling.

"I…I'm sorry."

Kelsie held up his hand. "Don't."

"No. I mean—"

"Dude? I just wanna chill."

"But."

Kelsie rolled to his side, his back facing Marty.

No, no, no…

Marty moved closer to the bed. "Let me explain."

"What's to explain? You don't want me. I get it."

Marty crept over the bed on his knees. "I don't –not-want you."

Kelsie didn't react.

"I mean, I might. I'm really cautious about it. I haven't been with a lot of guys before."

"Dude? I get it."

"I don't think you do." Marty felt sick to his stomach with worry. "I would kill to live happily ever after."

Kelsie glanced over his shoulder at him.

"I'm terrified of making a mistake."

As if his interest was piqued, Kelsie faced him, drawing a pillow under his head.

Marty sat on his heels and interlaced his fingers. "What if…what if I'm not enough for you? What if you think I'm a terrible lover and get repulsed by me? What if I don't make you happy? What will I do when you bring someone else back here to sleep with?"

Kelsie stared at him.

Marty whimpered. "I'm no good at stuff. I'm kind of a numbers guy."

"Hey." Kelsie reached out his hand. "It's okay."

"Now that you're rich you'll find someone who's wonderful. I'll be in the way. You'll ask me to move out. You'll ask me to live far away."

"Stop it. Marty. Come on."

Marty began to shake. "I can't make anyone happy. I tried to date before. I get scared. I freak them out. I need to be…" He felt his lip quiver.

"Need to be?"

"I need to be liked." He wanted to say 'loved'.

"I like you."

"Maybe I'm really ugly. Benjy didn't even kiss me. I mean, other than hello. On the cheek." He pointed to his face.

"Benjy and I didn't kiss."

Marty tried to stop his internal war and hear Kelsie. "Huh?"

"Kiss. Benjy and I. We fucked."

That confused Marty. "Wait. What?"

"I fucked him. That was it."

"Blowjob?"

"No."

"Hand-job?"

"No."

Nothing made sense to Marty. "He…you and he?"

Shrugging, Kelsie said, "He used to just get excited by me. I'd play my guitar for him and he'd clap and giggle, then yank his pants down, bend over, and invite me."

Marty struggled with the concept. "So, you just did it? Like, he made himself available and you did it?"

"Kinda." Kelsie propped his head up on his palm, lying on his side.

"Did you use protection?"

"Always. Dahhling! Never bare down there!"

"…'cause, ya know."

"I do know. Benjy got fucked a lot."

"Do you fuck a lot?" Marty asked.

"Are we going to discuss our sexual number?"

"Nope." Marty shook his head adamantly.

They both jumped when someone appeared at the doorway.

"Dinner is served."

Marty held his chest. "Thanks, Helga."

"Would you like to wait?" she asked.

"No. We're good." Kelsie sat up and placed his feet on the floor. "I sometime forget they're here," he whispered.

"I'm glad they are. I can't cook." Marty stood up, tucked his shirt in, and reached out his hand.

Kelsie clasped it, holding it, and they walked down the stairs to the dining room together.

~

Kelsie took his spot at the table as Marty joined him.

Helga brought two plates of salad out to them, smiling maternally as she did.

Kelsie looked for dressing on the table and there wasn't any. "Do you have that horseradish dressing?"

"The salad has vinaigrette on it," she said, "Taste it first?"

Feeling foolish, Kelsie stuck his fork into the lettuce and cucumber and ate it. "Mm." He nodded, liking the flavor. "It's good."

She smiled and asked, "Something to drink?"

Kelsie sat up higher and had a look at the ice water and juice already there. Kelsie sipped the water. "I'm good."

"Me too."

Helga acknowledged them and returned to the kitchen.

"Yummy salad." He poked his fork into something on his plate holding it up. "What's this?"

"Jicama." Marty ate a piece off his own plate.

"I don't know what that is." He held up another cube of something purple.

"Beet. Dude?" Marty laughed at him.

"Beets?" Kelsie made a face of fear.

Marty munched on a beet cube, one off his own plate.

Kelsie ate it. "Not bad."

"The dressing is to die for." Marty tore a roll in half and used it to mop up his plate.

Kelsie finished chewing and said, "I really like you, Marty."

"I really like you too, Kelsie."

Using his cloth napkin, Kelsie wiped his face and asked, "Do you like me enough to kiss me?"

"Yeah. I do." Marty's cheeks went crimson.

Testing the waters again, Kelsie leaned closer.

Marty met him halfway and kissed him.

"Awesome." Kelsie ate more jicama. "This is good."

"Yes. It is." Marty giggled.

THE ODD COUPLE

Chapter 10

Now it felt as if he and his best friend were together.

And that was pretty cool.

Marty ate the delicious food, feeling spoiled for the first time in his life.

Kelsie poked his fork into a scallop and held it up for Marty to eat.

"Mmm." He munched it and smiled, reciprocating with a shrimp from their main course, which was a seafood stew.

Kelsie ate it and then patted his belly. "I'm waving the white flag. I'm stuffed."

Helga must have heard because she came into the room. "I've made an apple crumble for dessert."

Marty was as full as Kelsie on the rich food. "You and Sigmund are too good at your jobs."

"Thank you." She began clearing the plates. "If you'd like, I can set the dessert to warm in the oven and you can help yourselves later."

"That sounds perfect." Kelsie sipped the ice water.

Knowing the married couple left after dinnertime, Marty tried to stack plates, making it easier for them to clear up, when Kelsie tapped him, gesturing to come with him.

Marty wiped his face and hands on his napkin and headed to the room at the end of the hallway.

Kelsie stood in the mauve space, the one Marty had selected to create their workout room. It had been cleared of the contents and sat empty. The room had a sliding glass door with a view of

97

the pool. "I was thinking mirrors on that wall. Matting on the floor…"

Marty was surprised Kelsie had given it any consideration at all.

"The bike and treadmill facing the patio. We can use that outlet." Kelsie pulled back the curtain. "The universal or free weights there."

Seeing Kelsie cared about what he was doing, Marty took the plunge. He went for Kelsie, intending on a nice kiss.

Catching Kelsie off balance, Marty held onto him as he fell back against the glass door with a bam! and hit the his head.

"Oh, my God!" Marty panicked. "I'm sorry!"

"Ow." Kelsie rubbed his head.

"Did you get hurt?" Marty rushed to inspect the back of Kelsie's head, running his hand over it lightly. "I'm so sorry!"

Kelsie recovered from the start, and stared at him.

Marty felt like a moron, until…

He was tackled to the floor and reached back to brace himself.

Kelsie landed on top of him and pinned him to the carpet.

Marty held Kelsie's shoulders, pushing him back until he let go of the terror, the apprehension of being close to this man. He gave in, submitting to Kelsie's dominance.

~

His act wasn't subtle.

Kelsie became aggressive and he knew in that moment, all of Marty's defenses broke down. Feeling Marty relax, spread his knees and open himself up for the taking, Kelsie began to go a little crazy.

Pent up from pleasing himself, especially since Benjy died, Kelsie craved sex and the touch of another man.

He pushed Marty's shirt up his chest, seeing his slender build and hairless torso. Running wide laps of his tongue along

Marty's skin, over his nipples and then sucking one, Kelsie wanted to come.

He knelt up, opened Marty's pants, and dragged them with his briefs down his hips.

~

Anticipating a bout of sweet kissing, maybe copping a feel, Marty was now at the mercy of an alpha wolf.

As his excitement elevated, so did his apprehension. Doubts formed. If he allowed Kelsie to take it all the first time they messed around, what was left?

Marty had been hurt too many times to admit.

Kelsie had a firm grip on his clothing, and yanked his pants down to his knees.

Marty's erect cock sprang out of his briefs.

Kelsie let go a low moan and dropped down on it, sucking it into his mouth.

Marty braced himself, both hands on the short pile rug. He stared at the ceiling and tried to recall the last time he received a blowjob, other than the brief one Kelsie had given him at the pool. His conscious thoughts were snapped out of his mind when the pleasure began to take over.

Using his saliva, Kelsie dampened Marty's dick and his ass, and worked both rigorously.

"Holy shit!" Marty clawed at the carpet and raised his hips off the floor, his back arching as the intensity rose.

Kelsie made a whimpering noise and penetrated Marty's ass with his fingertip.

Marty let go a howl of pleasure and came, his body nearly convulsing at the sensation of pure bliss.

Kelsie released his suction and cum spattered Marty's skin, the waves increasing as Kelsie milked him strongly, pulling on his erection.

Marty went limp on the carpet as he recovered. He felt a whoosh of air and lay still. "Oh, my God…" Marty held his chest as his groin reverberated from the thrill.

He touched his damp dick and stretched it, feeling sticky drops oozing out.

Stomping foot-patter returned, and Kelsie dropped to his knees on the floor and rolled Marty to his front, hoisting him to his hands and knees.

Marty gulped and spread his fingers on the mauve carpet. A condom wrapper hit the floor beside him and then Kelsie pushed in.

Marty choked and his brain began to go haywire.

~

A lubricated rubber on his dick, Kelsie gripped onto Marty's hips and pushed deeply into his ass. "Fuck yeah!" He was so pent up, he was riding the edge. A few quick trusts were all it took. He came and shivered down to his toes.

Closing his eyes, loving the tight heat, Kelsie moaned and then pulled out, falling onto Marty's back.

Marty dropped to the carpet and heaved for air under him.

"Oh, man. I think this has taken us to a whole new level of happiness."

Marty kept still.

Once he caught his breath, Kelsie managed to roll off of Marty and then he looked down at his sheathed cock. "Need tissues." He craned his neck to the attached bathroom. With an effort, Kelsie stood and headed to the bathroom, removing the condom and washing up, smiling at himself in the mirror.

~

So much for going slow.

Marty rolled to his back and touched his sticky skin. As was normal for him, he began to regret everything he had done to encourage this. Yet, in some place in his soul, he wanted it, wanted it so badly, he would beg.

But, now that they had sex, would Kelsie turn off?

He looked towards the bathroom and began to worry. Marty managed to sit upright and stared at his sticky skin, growing nervous and wondering if he had done the right thing.

Kelsie appeared, grinning happily and reached out his hand. "Need a boost?"

Marty took it, and Kelsie hauled him to his feet.

"That was so amazing. Wow." Kelsie was blushing, animated and back to himself.

Marty tried to smile in return and held his shirt up as he made his way to get clean.

~

Kelsie picked up the condom wrapper and brought it to the trashcan in the bathroom while Marty washed himself at the sink. He leaned against Marty's back and smiled at his reflection in the mirror. "Mm. What did you think? Huh? Nice?"

Marty turned off the tap and used a towel to dry himself, not answering.

"So, tomorrow, when the stuff arrives, do you think I had a good idea for placement?"

Marty stuck the hand towel into a hamper, and straightened his clothing.

"Dude?" Kelsie imagined they'd dance into the sunset.

Marty didn't meet his gaze, leaving the bathroom.

Confusion hit Kelsie. He shut off the light and followed Marty out of the room. "Did I do something wrong?"

"It's me." Marty headed up the stairs.

"What's you?" Kelsie didn't want to feel rejected, but he sure as hell did. "Are you saying, you didn't want to make love?"

"Can I have some alone time?"

"What? Oh. Sure." Kelsie paused on the top landing and watched Marty close himself into his room. He threw up his hands in frustration.

I can't do right! What the fuck?

Kelsie grew defensive and stood outside the closed door. "Ya could have said no! I didn't force you!"

Nothing was said from within.

Kelsie clenched his jaw in anger and stormed down the stairs. He opened the stove, seeing two helpings of apple crumble, took both of them out, burning his fingers. He shut off the stove, and then piled both desserts onto one plate, and brought the heaping mound to the game room.

He flopped onto a beanbag chair, pointed the remote at the screen for the TV, and ate the large helping, trying not to feel betrayed and bitter.

~

Marty wondered if his reaction was due to years of mistreatment.

What he anticipated, was a kiss. A get-to-know-you smooch. Maybe a little sexy tongue teasing.

He rolled to his side on the bed, tucking his hands between his knees, trying to understand his own reluctance.

There was nothing mean spirited here. No attempt at violating trust.

Why was he so confused?

He closed his eyes as fear of rejection hit. He'd been down this road before. So had Benjy.

Dahhling! We loved and loved and loved! Then? Nothing. No sex. Then, I find out he's jerking off to porn? I mean...isn't the real thing better?

"Sweet Benjy. I can relate."

THE ODD COUPLE

He stayed put for a while, thinking and trying hard not to over-think. But this was a familiar pattern.

He got up his courage, and climbed off the bed. Before he headed down the stairs, he looked at his phone. No messages.

Marty opened the oven and peeked inside. There were no desserts. And, the oven was cool. He foraged for something sweet and located the rest of the apple crumble in the fridge. After taking a portion for himself and heating it in the microwave, Marty had a feeling he knew where he'd find Kelsie.

Kelsie was splayed out on the floor, on top of two beanbag chairs, an empty plate with a fork lying beside him.

On TV was a war movie, not particularly Marty's taste. He sat on the hand-chair, which was becoming his favorite spot to hangout, and ate his dessert.

As Kelsie watched the big screen, he rubbed his belly as if he were full.

Marty figured Kelsie had eaten both of their desserts. He ate the sweet crumble quietly and then said, "I didn't mean to make you angry."

Kelsie ignored him.

"I just hoped we could work into it."

A loud exhale came from Kelsie, as if he were reluctant to discuss it.

"Fine. Give me the silent treatment. Be mad. It's what usually happens to me."

Kelsie turned to look at him. "You're a douche."

Marty winced, not expecting that harsh of a rebuking. He set the crumble down on the floor beside him, losing his appetite.

Kelsie seemed to watch the TV again and then he said, "You could have said no."

"I was afraid to upset you. I can't do anything right." He went to stand and bring his plate to the kitchen.

Kelsie rolled to his side to face him. "Why would I be upset? You do realize I'm not a moron. You can tell me to slow down."

"Slow down."

Kelsie rested his cheek on the beanbag chair and closed his eyes. "I'm so sick of games."

"I'm trying not to play them. Hey, all I wanted was to make out."

Kelsie raised his head off the chair. "Are you seventeen? What the fuck?"

Marty became insulted. "No! Just because I'm not a slut doesn't mean I'm immature." He picked up his plate.

~

Kelsie dreaded them becoming combatants. The way the will was worded, he and Marty could not sell, could not split the cash between them, nor could they benefit from any of Benjy's net worth without sticking together.

"And I'm sick of rejection." He watched Marty.

Marty paused, standing with the plate at the doorway. "I'm not rejecting you. I just wanted to go at a comfortable pace."

"Fine." Kelsie picked up his plate and held it up. "I ate two portions of that stuff. I'm about to puke."

Marty took Kelsie's plate and left the room.

Kelsie picked up the remote and shut off the TV, exhaustion beginning to hit. He got to his feet and looked for Marty.

He found him in the kitchen, hand-washing the plates at the sink. "Look, I'm sorry. I just...I thought you were into it."

Marty set the forks into the drain-board and dried his hands.

"Do you even think I'm cute?" Kelsie asked.

After placing the towel aside, Marty stared at him. "Yes. I think you're cute."

A little ray of hope opened up. Kelsie approached him, not touching him. "That's promising."

"Whatever happened to romance? Huh?" Marty asked, looking genuinely hurt.

"You mean, like roses and chocolates?"

"Yeah. Like that. Like wooing a partner, like waiting for the right time to make love." Marty tucked his shirt in. "What happened to it being special?"

"Okay." Kelsie shrugged, crossing his arms. "I guess you're in charge."

"Really? You'll let me set the pace?"

"Where am I going?"

Marty seemed to relax, letting go of his anxiety.

Kelsie leaned back on the kitchen counter, holding the edge with his hands. "I'm twenty-eight, Marty. I haven't dated anyone for any length of time. I lived on people's couches most of my adult life."

Marty pouted, staring at him with concern.

"I hate to admit I've even slept on the street. I'm not any good at being patient. I've learned to take things as I get them. If I don't, they sometimes vanish."

Marty seemed attentive, even understanding.

Kelsie hadn't revealed himself to anyone other than Benjy. Benjy knew he was on the street, knew he counted on the coins people tossed into his guitar case, knew he had slept in his car many nights.

No one else did.

~

This is what Marty had hoped for. Being real. Being truthful. The world was fraught with liars. Marty felt as if he was lucky enough to have met one man who was honest. Benjy Lloyd.

His faith in humanity, and that included family, had been destroyed. He wasn't close to anyone at the bank, didn't particularly like his boss, wasn't friends with his coworkers, he ate alone, he slept alone, he did his errands alone.

Being thrown into a situation where he had to be a partner, share his life, and become exposed was terrifying him.

But...

It had changed his reality. And Benjy had seen what Marty had, was indeed dismal.

Marty may have earned enough to rent an apartment, to buy a decent used car, but Marty was careful, too careful. He thought going out was wasteful and didn't like to pay for drinks in the bars in West Hollywood. Why pay for cocktails that were over ten dollars apiece? So? He was on his own.

Confronted with a young man who at first seemed to be his polar opposite, Marty began to peel back the layers.

Kelsie had built up a wall around him to protect himself.

They were both alone, both insecure, and both in need of something to cling to.

He opened his arms to his friend.

Kelsie went for that embrace and held tight.

Marty closed his eyes and rested his cheek on Kelsie's shoulder. All he wanted was to be loved. He had a lot of love in himself to give.

~

After Marty had gone to bed, Kelsie stayed up to watch a movie. Unfortunately, he chose a horror movie. And it freaked him the fuck out. He shut off the TV, then the light in the game room. Now that everyone had left and Marty was asleep, Kelsie tried not to let his imagination run wild. He made sure the doors were locked, but there were so many of them.

Sliding doors, a surveillance system, motion detection spotlights, even a guard patrolling the neighborhood.

THE ODD COUPLE

He stood at the slider in the kitchen, making sure the latch was turned. As he checked, he peered outside. Little solar lights were lit, guiding the way for anyone walking the path.

The pool glittered from the ambient light, the wind moving the surface.

Noises from the big house settling made Kelsie jump. He rubbed his arms from the chill and double-checked everything; from making sure he turned off the stove, to locking the front door.

Satisfied things were safe and secure, Kelsie climbed the stairs. He had a look both ways down the hallway from the top landing and shadows played tricks with his eyes.

Never should have watched a fucking horror movie.

Kelsie didn't usually like them, but against his better judgment he succumbed to the plot. It wasn't one of those slasher films, just a police drama with suspense and crime. That was enough for him to get anxious over.

He made his way to his master suite of rooms. Once inside, he turned on a light and stared at his bed, his guitar, and a pile of clothing he'd left on the floor. Kelsie entered the bathroom and illuminated the light over the vanity. At first he thought he saw someone in the room with him, then took a second look.

It was a towel lying over the shower door.

Damn. He held his chest and wished he wasn't so jumpy. Maybe it was the sugar in the apple crumble. He washed his face and brushed his teeth, meeting his green eyes in the mirror.

Every noise, every creek of the house made him shiver. He rinsed his mouth and wiped his face with a towel, then peeked into his bedroom.

"This is silly." He shook his head at himself, and shut off the bathroom light, undressing for bed. He had a peek at his phone, but no one had sent him any messages. The irony? Benjy had bought it for him, and paid his bill. He had also paid his car insurance for him.

Previous to meeting Benjy, Kelsie had been uninsured and rarely had money for gas. The only reason he moved his car was to prevent parking tickets and impounding.

Those days were gone.

He now lived in a nine-bedroom mansion and could drive a Bentley.

Kelsie dropped his clothing onto the pile on the floor and shut off the ceiling light, racing to the bed and hopping in, under the covers, pulling them over his head.

He curled into a tight ball and listened. The wind outside was making tree branches tap the glass.

Shaking off his fear, Kelsie exhaled and tried to relax.

When he did, he began to think about Benjy. He hadn't visited him when he became ill. The day he'd tried to see Benjy, the man himself had requested Kelsie remember him as he was.

The image in Kelsie's mind when he did recall Benjy, was of his robust laugh, his smile, and of course, his outlandish outfits and wild side.

As thoughts of Benjy surfaced, of Benjy's struggle to find a true heart, it gave Kelsie pause

Then, he heard a loud bang.

Kelsie froze and opened his eyes.

Another bang, as if a door was slammed, terrorized him.

"Nope. Uh-uh." He threw off the blanket, raced out of the room, and down the hall.

~

Marty felt the bed shift behind him. He gasped and sat upright, holding his chest.

"It's me. Don't kick me out."

"Are you okay?"

108

Kelsie scrambled to get under the blanket and held onto him. "I'm an idiot."

Marty relaxed beside him and felt Kelsie shivering. "Why?"

"I watched a stupid horror movie. Now I'm freaking out."

Marty snaked his arm around him and held on. "I hate movies like that."

"Me too. Never again." He rested his cheek on Marty's shoulder. "Sorry, dude."

It felt kind of nice to be the protector. "I've got ya." He chuckled.

A loud bang! made them both jump and cling together.

"What the hell is that?" Kelsie whimpered and gripped Marty in a death hold.

"It must be the house settling. We just moved in. We're getting used to it."

Another loud noise came from below.

"Dude!" Kelsie gasped. "Someone broke in?"

"But...we have an alarm. Did we set it?"

"I don't know. Did you set it?" Kelsie had his leg over Marty's.

"Um." Marty had no idea. He wondered if it was on a timer, or if Helga and Sigmund took care of it.

"We have to check." Kelsie didn't budge.

"Why?" Marty didn't want to check anything.

"What if someone's down there? Huh? What if they have a machete and come up here to hack us to pieces?"

"Don't watch those stupid movies anymore. No one's here." Marty could tell they were both listening.

"You do realize I won't sleep until we check," Kelsie whispered.

"Go. I'll wait here."

"No way, dude. You're coming."

Marty tried to tell if the noises had stopped. He held his breath.

Another creak came from what sounded like the stairs.

"He's coming up!" Kelsie burrowed under the blankets.

"You're freaking me out! Stop it. It's just the house."

"Go. Go look." Kelsie kept pushing him.

Marty had a feeling he wasn't going to get any sleep if he didn't. He nudged off the blanket and placed his feet on the carpet, still listening. "I need something to protect myself with."

"There's a high-heeled stiletto in the master bedroom closet."

"That's not even funny." Marty looked around the dark room. "I don't hear anything now."

"Go. Go!"

"Come with me!"

"Shhh!" Kelsie shook him. "Okay."

They climbed out of the bed and Marty dug through his closet, ending up with a short dowel, one from an unused clothing rack. He held it like a bat, and with Kelsie attached to his back, they tiptoed out of the bedroom.

On the top landing, they paused, looking down.

Marty was breathing so loudly he couldn't hear over it. "Are we searching all the rooms, or just the doors?"

"Fuck. I don't know."

"Fine." Marty, wanting to be the hero, the brave one, held the dowel up and made his way down the stairs. The house was dark, but he could see since his eyes had adjusted.

Feeling like a koala with a baby on its back, Marty first looked into the kitchen, seeing the sliding doors and the pool outside.

A loud noise made him and Kelsie jump out of their skin. It sounded as if something had hit the slider.

Marty went for the switch and the dining room was flooded with light. It was then, Marty could see bats flying around the pool, eating bugs.

Occasionally one would tap into the glass as if flew by.

He exhaled and lowered the dowel. "Bats."

"Bats?" Kelsie headed to the sliding door to look for himself.

Marty blinked when he realized Kelsie was naked.

"Cool! Shut the light." Kelsie stared outside.

Marty tapped the switch and stood beside him.

A flurry of night-feeders dive-bombed the moist air above the pool.

"Huh. Phew!" Kelsie made a cliché gesture of wiping off the sweat on his forehead.

"Right. Bed." Marty made his way back to the stairs.

"Are you sure that was it?" Kelsie followed.

"Yeah. Look." Marty pointed to the security pad near the front door. The panel was lit, showing the house was armed.

"You're a rock star." Kelsie smiled.

Not used to the praise, Marty smiled to himself and climbed up the flight of stairs back to his room. He set the dowel into the closet, relieved himself, and then returned to bed.

Seeing Kelsie in it made him happy.

They snuggled close under the blanket and Marty hugged him. "No more horror movies before bed."

"Swear to God." Kelsie kissed Marty's cheek.

"Goodnight, Kel."

"'Night, hero."

Marty sighed happily and fell asleep.

Chapter 11

Kelsie wasn't used to having a man sleeping beside him…in a clean bed, in a big mansion, after being well fed. Not only that, Marty was brave!

As the morning light began to filter into the room, he stirred from a restful slumber. Seeing Marty sleeping soundly beside him, Kelsie grew just a little more infatuated with him.

Yeah, they were different, yes, they didn't agree on everything, but…

He wasn't alone any longer.

The irony was the ties that bound him to this guy were set in stone. Yes. They were. If Kelsie left, if he tried to tear anything away from the estate, he'd get nothing.

Benjy had foreseen the future and if he and Marty did not get along, nothing from the inheritance would be given to them.

They either had to fall in love, or stomach living with someone they disliked…or…

Leave.

It was a risky plan, but so like-Benjy to have perpetrated it.

Maybe at first, Kelsie liked to annoy Marty. But it was his defense mechanism. If he irritated Marty, then it would make sense for Marty to dislike him.

If Kelsie didn't annoy him, and Marty didn't like him, well…it was because Kelsie wasn't likeable.

Hearing Marty's deep breathing beside him was comforting. He placed the pillow under his head and sighed, staring at

Marty's profile. He wouldn't classify Marty as a nerd, no. More of an anxiety-ridden nervous wreck…like him.

"Ha."

Marty's eyes opened and looked at Kelsie.

"Hello." Kelsie loved the blue color of Marty's irises.

"Hi." Marty stretched under the sheet. He looked towards the digital clock and then relaxed. "Wow. A Monday and I'm not obligated to go anywhere."

"I thought you were off Sundays and Mondays." Kelsie used one finger to brush the hair back from Marty's forehead.

"I need to clean my teeth." Marty covered his mouth.

"Okay."

Marty slid off the bed. He was wearing brightly printed pajamas, very much like Benjy's style. So much so, Kelsie had a feeling Marty had taken them from Benjy's belongings. It was sweet.

Before Kelsie commented on it, he noticed the material tenting over Marty's morning wood.

Marty entered the bathroom and closed the door.

"Good luck peeing with that." Kelsie rolled off the bed to go to his own room and wash up. He stared at his hard-on and chuckled, holding it while he walked.

~

Marty brushed his teeth and washed his face, then peed when his erection softened. He brushed his hair and opened the door to his bedroom to ask Kelsie something.

When he noticed the bed was empty, he was disappointed. Lowering his head, Marty undressed, preparing to shave and shower.

~

Kelsie cleaned his teeth and splashed his face. He checked his image out in the mirror and then left the bathroom, gathering fresh clothing into his arms. Last minute, he picked up the lube and condoms from his nightstand and as he returned to Marty's room he could smell food cooking and coffee brewing, as well as hear movement in the kitchen. Then, he heard the sound of a vacuum cleaner. So, the housekeeping crew had arrived.

He set his clothing on a chair and the items for lovemaking on the nightstand. Kelsie headed to the bathroom and peeked in. Marty was showering, having already shaven at the sink.

Kelsie smiled in delight. He moved the shower door back and watched Marty clean up. "Damn, you're hot."

Marty startled at the comment and turned around to see him. "Oh. Hi."

"Hi." Kelsie tried to be good. Tried to wait for an invitation.

As if Marty could see right through him, he chuckled. "Do you want to join me?"

Kelsie brightened up. "Should I get a rubber?" The minute the fun left Marty's expression, Kelsie figured the comment was too pushy. He climbed in and tried to keep his hands to himself.

After Marty shifted in the stall to allow Kelsie the chance to stand under the spray, Marty asked, "Can't we just kiss?"

"Kiss? Naked in the shower?" Kelsie wetted down and used soap that was in a wall dispenser.

"Never mind." Marty made a move to get out of the tub.

Kelsie touched his shoulder, getting his attention. Marty met his gaze and stared at him.

Slowing down to allow Marty his chance at romance, Kelsie nodded and tried not to push him.

The light returned to Marty's eyes as he closed the gap between them.

Kelsie felt his cock engorge while Marty touched his chin, going for a kiss. At the press of their lips, Kelsie's urge to bend Marty over and fuck him, grew.

To stop himself from doing the wrong thing, Kelsie interlaced his hands behind his own back and closed his eyes.

Marty parted his lips and ran light swirls of his tongue against his.

Kelsie whimpered and did something he rarely had done, he let go. He shut down his own urges and defenses and allowed Marty to lead.

~

It wasn't mission impossible.

Kelsie could be tamed. Couldn't he?

Marty enjoyed the slow rapture, the dancing of their tongues and the chills it sent over him.

As the hot water created swirls of steam around them, Marty enjoyed that kiss. Enjoyed it very much.

He felt Kelsie shift, resting his back on the marble wall of the stall. Marty peeked at him, seeing Kelsie had placed his hands behind his back, as if he were restraining himself.

Marty parted from the sensual kiss, seeing its effect. "That wasn't so bad, was it?"

Kelsie made a low moan of longing.

Marty finished in the shower, and Kelsie faced the spray to shampoo his hair. After he climbed out, Marty rubbed a towel across his back and over his hair, smiling at himself in the mirror.

When he heard grunting, Marty turned to look. Kelsie was jerking himself off.

His smile fell. He rolled back the door. "Really? Can't let it build?"

"Huh?" Kelsie looked at him from over his shoulder. "What? I can't jerk off either?"

Marty slid the shower door closed and left the bathroom. "This is absurd."

~

Kelsie stopped jerking himself and watched Marty leave. He shut off the water and moved back the sliding door. "I can't?"

115

When he didn't get an answer he stepped out of the tub, wrapped a towel around his back and saw Marty getting dressed. "Dude? I don't know the rules."

"It's okay." Marty's body language told Kelsie it was not okay.

"Hey. I won't. I didn't think it was a big deal."

Marty stopped what he was doing and faced him. "It's not up to me to tell you what to do. I guess this wasn't meant to be."

"No. Hang on." Kelsie touched Marty's arm. "I didn't know. So, no jerking off?"

Marty, wearing just his jeans, sat on the bed.

Kelsie sat beside him. "I can't read your mind. Maybe Benjy could, but I'm struggling here."

"I just…" Marty rubbed his face. "I have this image in my head. It's farfetched. I know."

Kelsie used the edge of the towel to dab at the water running from his wet hair. "Can ya at least tell me?"

After releasing a loud exhale, Marty said, "I imagined us being celibate, of letting it build. And then…then!" Marty smiled as if he were divulging the secrets of the universe. "Then, we finally find our pleasure. We make wonderful love."

Kelsie sort of got it. "And, how long is this letting-it-build stage?"

"Do we have to have a timeline?"

"If you're talking about me not being able to jerk off, yes."

"You can't go without?"

"I can. Why should I? I can't jerk off at all?"

"Never mind." Marty went to stand.

"Hang on!" Kelsie tugged him back to the bed. "Why can't you talk to me? You keep telling me how great Benjy was to talk to. I want to be that guy."

Marty settled down again. "I don't have a specific timeline. Just, can we make it romantic?"

"You're really hung up on that romance shit. Okay." Kelsie stood up and used the towel to dry his hair.

~

Marty stared at Kelsie's cock.

It was tempting. Even soft, Kelsie's cock hung past his balls, the head a perfect mushroom shape, and the man did not shave his pubic hair.

Guilt hit Marty. He shouldn't be the one to make demands.

This is why I struggle. I have unreal expectations.

Kelsie walked back to the bathroom.

Marty watched him, seeing his tight ass and narrow hips.

He had to meet Kelsie halfway. It wasn't fair, was it?

Marty flopped back on the bed and stared into space. In reality, he had no idea what he wanted. But one thing was certain, he couldn't have everything.

~

As Kelsie changed into clean clothing Marty waited for him. Nodding he was ready, they headed down the stairs to see the lower level being mopped, dusted, vacuumed, and polished.

Kelsie paused to look at the pool, which since it had just been serviced, was clean and inviting.

The entire estate was maintained by an efficient team; and that included laundry and changing sheets and towels.

Kelsie had somehow gone from living on the streets, or an occasional seedy motel, to a mansion. He stopped asking himself why he deserved it.

He spun around to find Marty already in his place at the table, sipping coffee as Helga brought out a bowl of freshly cut fruit, including kiwi, ruby grapefruit, raspberries, and pineapple.

Seeing yoghurt and granola on the table, and Marty using a spoon to plop a dollop on his fruit, and sprinkle granola on top, Kelsie did the same. He ate a mouthful and moaned. "Damn."

Marty chuckled.

Helga made sure the coffee pot was on the table, and then asked, "Pecan waffles, challah French toast, or eggs?"

"Wow! Pecans? Yes, please." Kelsie kept devouring his fruit.

"Sounds good." Marty smiled at her.

She perked up to the noise of the housecleaners, closed a paneled divider to separate them from it, and returned to the kitchen where Sigmund was working.

Kelsie glanced at the couple and then said, "I love them."

Marty agreed, his cheeks full of fruit. "They go to fresh markets daily." He swallowed his mouthful. "Benjy told me they try to buy locally. That's why everything tastes so good."

"Maybe we can plant a garden."

Marty perked up. "Yes! I've lived in an apartment most of my life. I would love a garden! Herbs, veggies!"

"We can try."

"Our gym equipment is coming today." Marty poured cream into his coffee cup.

"So many things to do." Kelsie popped a grape into his mouth.

Marty took a look into the kitchen, stretching to make sure no one could overhear, and then whispered, "I'm sorry I let you down."

Kelsie turned his attention towards him. "You mean the bats?"

"No." Marty lowered his voice. "The jerking off. I was out of line. I can't tell you when to do that."

"You're right." Kelsie smiled.

"Oh?"

"You can't." Kelsie chuckled.

"Oh."

Kelsie finished his fruit and licked the yoghurt off the spoon. "I need to come at least once a day. Don't you?"

"I can. I mean…" Marty's cheeks went rosy. "I don't. But I can."

"I can and I do." Kelsie drank the creamy coffee. "I used to have to sneak it. Ya know, when I lived at other people's places. Usually in the shower."

Marty held his cup in both hands. "So, you've never had your own place?"

"No."

"It's tough. LA's really expensive. I didn't realize it until I came here. I almost didn't make it. I was ready to move back to Spokane. I just didn't want to."

"Reno had cheap places. I guess I could have stayed there. I just got sick of it."

They both stopped talking when Helga brought out two plates of food. Crusty brown waffles, topped with pecans and powdered sugar. She, then, brought out a small warmed pitcher of maple syrup as well as creamery butter.

"Damn." Kelsie doused his waffles with loads of butter and syrup.

Marty poured the syrup to the side and dipped each bite. "Holy cow." He moaned at the taste.

"What time is the equipment coming?" Kelsie said, chewing.

"The last time I looked, it read just by the end of the day. No exact time."

Kelsie nodded. "I don't suppose it matters."

"Nope." Marty picked up a pecan and ate it.

Kelsie paused a moment. "We're really lucky, Marty."

"I know." Marty's expression became serious.

"I mean it. I never in my life expected this."

Marty said, "Me neither."

Kelsie set his fork down and stared at the pool, which was glistening in the sunshine. "I wish I could have said goodbye. I wish he'd have told me. I never thanked him."

"How were we supposed to know?" Marty sliced a piece of waffle. "He never made any indication of his intentions to me when he was alive."

"No. To me either."

He and Marty stared at each other.

"Can I have a kiss?" Marty asked.

Kelsie leaned closer for that kiss.

After, Marty smiled, and his eyes shined brightly. "Thank you."

Kelsie went back to eating his waffles, liking the sweetness of Marty's little kisses.

~

Since it appeared Monday was the big day of the week for cleaning, laundry, and maintenance, Kelsie opted for the relative quiet near the pool. He sat on the edge, kicking his feet in the water, sunglasses on his nose, as butterflies, appearing drunk on nectar, spun in dizzying circles.

The slider opened and Marty emerged, holding his laptop. He sat beside him on the pool ledge, but cross-legged. "I looked up gardens."

Kelsie took an interest.

"Right." He held the tablet on his leg. "Regarding creating a garden. We need to pick a spot with bright sun. Then, dig up a section, use fertilizer on it, aerate it..." He bit his lower lip as he read from the screen. "Then, choose the plants, or seeds, plant them in rows..."

Kelsie leaned on his hands, looking at his feet as he pulled them to the surface and wriggled his toes.

"Um...make an irrigation system...we can use hoses that soak the ground...then keep the bugs and animals from eating them with natural methods—"

"Marty?"

"Yeah?"

"How about a planter box on the patio with herbs?"

Marty looked at the tablet solemnly. "I can do it. What else will I have to do? I'm going to lose my mind."

"Have you heard anything from the bank since you quit?"

"No." Marty used his finger on the tablet and scanned social networks.

Kelsie leaned on his shoulder to see the screen. Marty had a meme of a rainbow as his profile photo, and ten friends. Kelsie didn't care much about owning a computer or a phone. They served to remind him of what he didn't have. A social life and friends.

Marty shut down the computer and stretched to set it on a glass and iron table. He then stuck his feet into the pool. He was wearing shorts.

"Was brave of you to use a rainbow." Kelsie looked out at the view.

"Nah. I didn't post any of my information. So, no one from Spokane would figure out it's me."

Kelsie didn't comment, trying to chill, since he'd spent twenty plus years stressing, hungry, and lonely.

"Are you okay?" Marty bumped him with his shoulder.

"I was told I'm manic. Maybe. I don't know."

"Do you go up and down?"

"Sometimes." Kelsie used his toes to reach a beach ball which was floating in the water, and tapped it closer so he could pick it up.

"Ya know. I used to wonder about Benjy. About what he did all day." Marty kicked his feet lazily in the warm water.

"He volunteered. He used to do a lot of stuff." Kelsie threw the ball at his feet and tried to bounce it back to himself.

"He did?"

"Yeah. Soup kitchens, LGBT centers...stuff like that." Kelsie shook the water off the ball, set it on his lap and rested his chin on it.

"Huh. How come I didn't know?"

The slider opened behind them.

They both turned to look.

Helga was there. "Your equipment has arrived."

"Oh!" Marty stood and took a towel off a stack, rubbing his legs dry.

Kelsie didn't move. He sighed.

"Do you want to help?" Marty asked him.

"Is it okay if I don't?"

"Sure."

Kelsie pressed his cheek to the plastic ball, hearing the slider open and close. He stared at tall palm trees swaying in the wind, and shut his eyes.

Chapter 12

After two hours, Marty realized he was driving the two delivery guys out of their minds.

They had moved the equipment so many times, they were dripping with sweat.

It hit Marty. His OCD was becoming their problem, and that wasn't right.

The irony was, now the items were where Kelsie had suggested, and it was by far, the best placement.

"Okay." Marty gave up. "It's fine."

As a gesture of kindness, and perhaps thankfulness that Marty was done, they plugged the machines in.

Marty removed his wallet and took out all the cash he had left in it. He handed it to the guy closest to him. "Thanks. Sorry."

The man took it, folding the bills and tilted his head for his partner to go. They removed the packaging and boxes, taking them with them.

Marty gave the room a last look, and then followed the men to the front door.

~

After the noise of the landscaper using a leaf blower chased him away from the pool, Kelsie sat on the trunk of his car with his guitar. Avoiding the chaos of noise, the cleaning, folding of laundry and gym setup, he needed to find peace.

When the front door opened, he noticed the two men from the shipping company leave, shaking their heads and giving each other looks of exasperation as they removed large boxes, folded flat.

Kelsie could only imagine what Marty had put them through. He stayed where he was until they drove the truck off the property, and then he slid off his trunk. He was thinking about going into the house, but the cleaners were still there, so that meant noise.

Kelsie opened the back door of his car, setting his guitar into it, and then entered the garage. He turned on the overhead lights, seeing fluorescent bulbs flicker and illuminate.

Two cars were inside the building, the Bentley, and a Maserati. The rest of the space was open, except for boxes and plastic storage bins.

There were so many nooks and crannies to explore in this mansion, Kelsie wondered if he would ever have the energy to dig through all of the items Benjy had accumulated.

He touched the gleaming fenders as he passed, and then stood in front of a wall of shelves.

Box after box of holiday decorations were there.

He knew from past experience, Benjy did the home up to the extreme for both Halloween and Christmas.

Kelsie opened the bins and boxes, seeing lawn displays, inflatable santas and jack-o'-lanterns, witches, goblins, elves and fake evergreen trees.

He located another box and inside it were gory mechanical creatures, electronic robots that Benjy used during his parties for the bewitching day.

A tombstone was among the collection. It read, 'I told you I was sick'.

Kelsie's smile fell.

He closed the top and backed away. "Stop haunting me!"

His voice echoed in the garage, and he realized how idiotic he sounded. Benjy wasn't haunting him. He was haunting Benjy.

THE ODD COUPLE

~

"Kel?" Marty looked for his housemate. He checked the pool, then jogged up the stairs. "Kelsie?"

The cleaning crew was inside the master bathroom at the moment. Marty took a look into the many rooms on the top floor, then became confused. He trotted back downstairs, left through the slider, and searched the side of the house.

It was then he spotted a padlock on the fence, one that had been used to stop trespassers. He stood on his toes to see over the gate, and then returned to the house.

In the noise of vacuuming and scrubbing, Kelsie had left. Marty opened the front door to see if a car was missing. His and Kelsie's were parked where they had left them last week. He walked to the garage and realized a light was on inside it.

"Kel?" He peeked in. Both cars were there. He was about to keep looking for Kelsie elsewhere when he saw boxes were standing open on the far side of the detached building.

Marty took a look beyond the two cars to see if Kelsie was there. He was.

Relieved to find him, Marty was going to ask him to check on the exercise room when he noticed Kelsie seemed to be out of it.

He was crouching, his back to one cement wall, staring into space.

"Hey." Marty walked closer. "What did ya find?" He glanced at the boxes.

Kelsie rubbed his eyes roughly with the backs of his hands.

"Kel?" Marty became concerned. "Are you okay?"

Kelsie looked up at him. "He was good to me, but I was a shitty friend to him."

"No. No way. Why would he leave the house to you? Nope." Marty had a peek at what Kelsie had found to bring on this pensive mood. He could see Christmas decorations, as well as Halloween.

125

"Look at all this stuff!" Marty opened the box tops to inspect the contents. He then, spotted a headstone, a lawn decoration. Seeing what was written on it made his heart stop.

He looked back at Kelsie. "You didn't know he was ill. Neither did I."

Kelsie kept wiping at his eyes.

Marty approached him. "Hey."

Kelsie burst into tears and lurched up to hug Marty.

Marty rocked him, squeezing him close. Kelsie's anguish made him weepy as well. "Did ya cry before today?"

He felt Kelsie nod his head.

As he rubbed Kelsie's back, trying to comfort him, Marty said, "He had a private death. I don't know if anyone was with him when he died or when he was sick. I'm clueless."

"Me too." Kelsie inhaled and released him, using the tail of his shirt to wipe his face.

"He wasn't buried. I read in the paper he was cremated. That much I know."

"His ashes?"

"Scattered on the Hollywood sign. With pink glitter."

Kelsie made a noise, a mix of a sob and a laugh.

"He loved you." Marty put his arm around Kelsie.

"I loved him." Kelsie slowly controlled himself.

"That's the funny thing about people. You don't always know what you have until they're gone."

"I need to get out of here."

Marty glanced back at the boxes, and then walked with Kelsie to the door. He shut lights, closed the door behind him, and he and Kelsie returned to the house.

The cleaning crew was finally through, packing their van.

Kelsie removed his guitar from the back seat of his car, and then the two of them entered the house.

It was blissfully quiet.

THE ODD COUPLE

Kelsie headed up the stairs, while Marty entered the bathroom closest to the kitchen, washing his hands. He looked into the mirror, seeing his expression and the sadness in it. He held the sink and battled back the sorrow.

~

Kelsie set his guitar into the case and snapped it closed.

He washed his hands in the master bathroom, seeing everything sparkling and clean. Fresh towels, new soap, polished fixtures, and laundered mats.

Kelsie wondered if he and Marty were chosen because they loved Benjy. Loved him so much.

"Thank you." Kelsie stared at the ceiling. "I mean it."

~

Marty stood at the doorway of the room with the exercise machines in it. He hoped, like with so many people, he and Kelsie didn't end up avoiding the workout. As he imagined getting a flat screen TV and music system, Marty touched the shining new free weights, all in a row, on a long metal rack.

He picked up one, did a curl and set it back down quickly. "I have no idea what I'm doing."

What now? Get a trainer? Where does it end?

He sank to the floor and crossed his legs, feeling numb. Working full-time had been exhausting.

Was not working exhausting too?

When he worked as a teller, he may not have been rich, but he wasn't miserable.

He also wasn't materialistic.

He should just be grateful. Was that too much to ask?

~

After getting his emotions under control, Kelsie looked for Marty. He peeked into his bedroom, then headed down the stairs. Hearing Helga and Sigmund preparing lunch, Kelsie glanced outside onto the patio and then made his way down the long hallway.

Marty was there, sitting cross-legged on the carpet in the middle of the equipment.

The room had been setup the way he suggested it, and it shocked him. "Wow."

Marty looked up at him.

"This is outstanding." He inspected each item, and then the free weights. He did a few curls and set the dumbbell down. "We need tunes."

"Yes." Marty nodded, appearing spent or tired.

Kelsie sat next to him, stretching out his legs, with his hands behind him, propping him up. "You did a good job."

"Thanks."

"We should pick a specific time of day to do it. Like eleven. Something like that."

"I don't know how."

"I know enough." Kelsie sat up and studied Marty. "I'm sorry for the meltdown. But, I guess it was inside me. It was bound to come out."

"It's okay. We can miss him."

"What do you think Helga and Sig are making for lunch?" He tried to snap them out of their mood. "Maybe we should ask for low calorie food."

Marty met his gaze.

"Man, you have the bluest eyes."

Marty touched Kelsie's cheek.

"Can I kiss you?" Kelsie asked.

"Yes."

Kelsie inched closer, and closed his eyes. As their lips met, he had the urge to pin Marty to the floor and ravish him.

While they swirled tongues, Kelsie got a hard-on and had no idea what to do with his hands.

Marty cupped the back of his head, making little whimpering noises.

Kelsie parted from the kiss and licked his lip, staring at the bulge in Marty's shorts.

When he felt Marty's caress on his cheek, he met his gaze. Marty drew him back for more kisses. It drove Kelsie crazy. As he began to roll them over, so he could lie on top of Marty, Kelsie stopped himself and remained on his side, only touching Marty's shoulder.

Then, it was as if the kissing had a life of its own.

While they explored each other's mouths, teased with their tongues, and nibbled each other's lips, Kelsie felt as if he had missed out. Missed out on 'romance' and maybe, just maybe, he had never felt it before.

Sex was not romance. Nor was it love.

With Marty leading the way, Kelsie enjoyed the kisses. That's all they were doing. Kissing. Not groping, not grinding, not anything.

When Marty parted from the kiss, he smiled lovingly at Kelsie.

"That was amazing." Kelsie loved it.

"You're a great kisser."

"I am?" Kelsie touched Marty's cheek with the back of his finger.

"You are."

Kelsie closed his eyes and wanted more.

~

This is what he was missing.

The sweetness and innocence of first love. To Marty, the journey to find 'the one' wasn't a fuck. Wasn't a hookup.

Yes, he was excited, of course, he was hard, absolutely it would be cool to come, but...

How rich and velvety were these kisses?

They were intoxicating.

Marty admired Kelsie for his willpower. He expected Kelsie to pin him to the floor, to grab his cock, to do all sorts of things to him.

They would.

If they desired each other, then, a natural flow would occur.

Marty ended their kiss and stared into Kelsie's eyes. They were green. Green and a little gold.

He touched the beard growth on Kelsie's jaw, feeling its softness.

"You drive me crazy."

"That's a really good thing." Marty touched Kelsie's lower lip with the tip of his finger.

"I have a confession."

"You're straight," Marty teased.

"Ha. No." Kelsie propped his head up in his palm, his elbow on the floor. "I hate admitting I was wrong."

"Oh?" Marty drew a line up Kelsie's jaw to his cheekbone.

"This is very cool." Kelsie smiled as Marty showed him what real romance was all about. "I think I know why I missed out before."

"Why?" Marty traced Kelsie's eyebrows.

"Time. I never had the comfort of it. We do now."

"We do. Neither of us is going anywhere, are we?"

"Benjy saw to that. Man, did he know me."

"I want to know you like Benjy did. Only better."

Kelsie urged Marty into more kisses.

Chapter 13

How long did they lay on the floor in the middle of their new workout room?

Kelsie didn't know.

But, he did know, he enjoyed every second. Where did he have to go? Nowhere.

He and Marty had time, and that was a huge luxury.

They parted from the kissing and smiled, then laughed.

And, as if she'd been waiting for them to come up for air, Helga said softly from the hallway, "Lunch is ready."

Kelsie craned his neck to see her, looking at her upside down. "Did Benjy teach you timing?"

"He did." She smiled and walked off.

Marty got to his feet and reached down. Kelsie clasped his hand and was helped up, and they continued to hold hands as they walked towards the dining room.

"Do we need to tell her about our low calorie menu?" Marty asked.

"Nah." Kelsie chuckled. "The food is too good to mess with."

"I've never eaten like this, have you?"

"Hell no. I couldn't afford to."

"Even if I could, I wouldn't have before."

Kelsie nudged Marty to enter the dining room first, seeing fresh flowers on the table as well as the usual elegant china place settings. They sat down and Helga brought out bagels, sliced and on a platter, then smoked fishes, cream cheese, capers and paper-thinly sliced red onion.

131

Marty selected a bagel. "They're warm."

"I love you, Helga!" Kelsie chuckled as he took a seeded bagel to his plate.

"I love you too!" she sang.

Kelsie picked up the serving fork and before he took a helping of smoked salmon and trout, he noticed Marty giving him a lovesick smile. They stretched towards each other and kissed.

"Fucking awesome." Kelsie filled his bagel with the goodies and grew excited at where he and Marty would go next in their relationship.

~

After lunch, Kelsie challenged Marty to an air-hockey game. They played in the game-room, slamming the puck into the sides to bank it and slip through the slot.

Kelsie was by far the aggressor in the match, but Marty's patience, and his aim, were paying off.

After each score, one celebrated while the other booed.

It was as if Marty could finally live his childhood. Most of his life he'd been timid, afraid, and never allowed himself to let go.

"Yes!" Kelsie did a victory dance and spun around.

"Best of nine?" Marty tossed the puck on the table.

"Nope. You said best of seven a minute ago." Kelsie shook his head. When the music stopped, Kelsie tapped the jukebox buttons and another song played; Herman's Hermits, '*I'm into something good.*'

Though he hadn't been a fan of sixties music, Marty was becoming one.

He and Kelsie began to do the twist and faced each other, dancing and laughing.

"Now this is a workout!" Kelsie kept twisting, his bare feet pivoting on the carpet.

"Benjy would be so proud!" Marty held his arms over his head and kept up the dance, since the song seemed to be perfect for it.

Kelsie whooped it up and they began to do silly things, like the shimmy and shake, and the hula-hoop. When the song ended, Kelsie dropped onto a beanbag chair and laughed his head off.

Marty was glistening in sweat as he peered through the curved glass of the jukebox to see what else there was to play. "I only know a few of these bands. Wow. This is like music history 101."

"Benjy was so cool. Look at this room. Lava lamps, that hand-chair, the beanbags. I mean, groovy, dude."

"Oh, my God! Do you remember that go-go getup he had? With the white lipstick and big hoop earrings?"

"Dahhling!" Kelsie held up an invisible cocktail. "Are you a mod or a rocker? I'm a cocker!"

"He must have that outfit somewhere." Marty landed on the second beanbag chair and it made a loud squishy noise.

Kelsie rolled over to face him. "Hey. Did you find his computer?"

"No. Did he have one?"

"He must have had one." Kelsie appeared deep in thought.

"Maybe he asked someone to get rid of it. Can you imagine what would be on Benjy's computer?"

"I already saw his porn collection." Looking towards the TV cabinet, Kelsie exaggerated a shiver.

Marty was having so much fun, he scooted closer to Kelsie, thinking he was sexy as hell, especially when he was doing the twist with him.

"Uh-oh." Kelsie smiled, a devilish gleam in his eyes.

Marty ran his finger down Kelsie's shoulder to his elbow.

"That just made me tingle." Kelsie moaned in ecstasy.

"Come 'ere." Marty craned his finger.

Kelsie eagerly rolled to his side and faced him.

"Wait." Marty knelt upright, pushed two buttons on the jukebox, and then settled down mirroring Kelsie's position on the floor.

The Monkees' '*Daydream believer*' played.

Kelsie touched himself, drawing Marty's eye. Yup. They were both excited, and this was fun. He went for a kiss.

Kelsie embraced him, but...didn't do what Marty expected, which was roll on top of him to pin him to the floor.

The man may be crazy, but he was a fast learner.

Marty fell just a little bit in love at that very moment.

~

Kelsie felt his cock throbbing and he was going crazy. Crazy in a good way. This new romance stuff was pretty fantastic.

And if it meant, doing things together with Marty, things he'd never done before, he was down with it.

Letting Marty lead, letting someone else decide, was exciting him to a new high.

Then, it occurred to Kelsie, Benjy had been the one to decide for him as well. He would never have taken for granted anything with Benjy.

It was always Benjy who initiated sex, who yanked his own clothing down and invited Kelsie in.

And Benjy never had sex with Marty...wow.

When he heard himself whimper, Kelsie couldn't recall doing that, or being this excited by a partner while simply kissing.

It was Marty who initiated more contact. He touched Kelsie's neck, right at his T-shirt's crewneck and traced a line down Kelsie's chest.

Kelsie didn't reciprocate, spreading and closing his fingers as Marty brought him to new heights in foreplay.

Slowly, Marty tugged Kelsie's shirt up, then he ran light finger touches across Kelsie's skin.

THE ODD COUPLE

As he huffed for air, Kelsie parted from the kiss and kept still, wanting Marty to continue exactly what he was doing.

~

Marty was impressed. He had no idea when he had asked Kelsie to slow down, that Kelsie was a man of his word.

With the lightest tickling strokes, Marty made circles around Kelsie's erect nipples and down his treasure trail. He could see his chest rise and fall rapidly, and he knew he was driving Kelsie crazy.

While Davy Jones' vocals floated through the air, Marty drove Kelsie out of his mind. He stared at the bulge in Kelsie's shorts and admired the outline of his erection. Marty held up Kelsie's shirt and ran kisses from his sternum to his belly button.

Kelsie rolled to his back, bent his knees, and spread his legs.

Marty envisioned them making love; next time it will be slow, affectionate love, and that thought inspired him.

The sex acts they had done previously began to become meaningless. It was the equivalent of a hookup in Marty's mind. Which meant basically, coming with another man, without any emotional attachment.

It wasn't something Marty aspired to, ever. He was twenty-five and wanted to be loved. Loved for who he was, warts and all.

Of course there was a temptation to touch Kelsie's dick, to cup that attractive mound under his zipper flap.

Instead, he backed off, relaxing on his side, staring at Kelsie. Benjy had obviously seen the potential of the two of them succeeding. The irony to Marty was, he had never met Kelsie before the reading of the will.

Kelsie made a move as if he was going to touch himself, but instead, he mirrored Marty's position and they locked gazes.

Marty smiled, thinking about how adorable his housemate was.

The song ended and the house became completely silent. Helga and Sigmund had left to buy fresh ingredients for dinner, and finally, the entire grounds and cleaning crew, had departed.

It was just the two of them.

"What now?" Kelsie asked.

Marty inched closer and embraced him, resting his cheek on Kelsie's shoulder. Kisses touched Marty's hair and Kelsie rubbed his back lovingly.

He felt safe in Kelsie's arms.

~

Kelsie stared at the ceiling as Marty snuggled with him. As their relationship morphed from adversarial, to complicated, to simple, Kelsie began to appreciate Benjy's foresight.

Never, would he have imagined a man like Marty as a boyfriend. No, not just a sex partner, a real boyfriend. One he'd commit to, one he'd be happy with for any length of time.

Sure, there was no way to predict the future, but Benjy had most certainly thought this one out.

You don't leave your estate to two guys who have never met without either a wicked sense of humor or intuition.

Benjy had both.

"Can I ask you something?" Kelsie rested his hand on Marty's back.

"Yes."

"We slept together and I really liked it." He felt Marty shift over him. "I mean, the sleeping."

"Still listening."

"This place is big, and scary."

"Yeah. It is."

"So, if I promise not to do anything you don't want, can we sleep in the same room?"

"Okay."

"That was easy." Kelsie smiled.

136

"I can't have you losing sleep because of bats."

Kelsie chuckled. But soon, his smile faded. "I've been on my own for so long. I get really lonely."

Marty leaned up so they could see each other. "Me too."

"Are we weird? I mean, everyone else seems to have a huge network of friends."

"Maybe." Marty shrugged. "I don't feel comfortable with crowds. And, most people have let me down."

Kelsie had similar feelings. Maybe they were different at first glance, but the more Kelsie learned about Marty, the more common ground he found they had. And being a loner and isolated, was a big similarity.

"I had a thought." Kelsie cupped Marty's cheek. "What if we hated each other? Can you imagine?"

"Benjy made sure we couldn't split this place up."

"He did. It was do or die. I really thought the two of us were going to end up painting a white line down the middle of the house."

Marty smiled at him. "So did I."

"He knew. Somehow he knew."

"He hoped. Let's not forget how many times Benjy had his heart broken."

Kelsie stared into space. "Yet, he kept trying. You have to give him credit. He was still in the game even after so many disasters."

"A lesser man would have given up. I would have."

"What will happen if we don't manage to stay happy together?"

"I guess we'll deal with it." Marty touched the cotton fabric of Kelsie's shirt.

"I don't want other guys coming here to see you." Kelsie already felt possessive.

"Who the hell's coming to see me?" Marty made a noise as if it was absurd.

Kelsie snaked his arm around Marty and drew him close, afraid of screwing it up and being at odds again.

"I think Benjy had lousy taste in men. And, I'm talking about the ones he dated."

"Does that include me?" Kelsie asked.

"You two dated?"

Kelsie's first response was no, but it gave him pause.

Marty shifted back so they could see each other's eyes again. "I thought you said you just fucked."

"We did. But, if we had sex and also had a decent time when we didn't fuck...and if he was helping me with some stuff—"

"Benjy helped you? Financially?"

Seeing something turn off in Marty, Kelsie became hesitant.

"What did he pay for?" Marty indeed seemed upset.

"Don't back off. Hang on." Kelsie tried to keep Marty close.

"No. Let go." Marty sat upright on the floor. "You took money from him?"

Kelsie sat on one of the beanbags. "Are you really arguing with me about it when you're now living off of him?"

"That's not the same."

"Why are you turning this into a fight?"

"What did he pay for? Can't you tell me?"

"My car insurance and my phone."

"Oh."

"Oh." Kelsie became offended. "And I never asked. Never."

Marty appeared to give it thought.

Kelsie became irritated. He stood up and tugged at his shirt, making it lay over his pants. "I was living in my car most of the time. He kept it from being impounded."

Marty stared at him.

138

"Ya wanna tell me how I should have had a real job? Huh? You want to lecture me like my father did? Go ahead."

"I'm not going to do that."

"I didn't ask him for a fucking thing." Kelsie made his way to the doorway.

"Kel. Hang on."

He turned to look at Marty, furious with him.

"I judged you. I'm sorry."

"You wanted to know how life was going to be in this house if we fought. Keep accusing me of using Benjy and you'll find out."

"I'm sorry. Kel. I am." Marty reached out to him.

Kelsie nodded, as if accepting the apology, but he didn't hang around. He walked off, already feeling guilty for everything Benjy had done for him. He didn't need someone else laying that trip on him.

~

Marty cursed himself for starting trouble. It wasn't up to him to decide what Benjy had done or whom he had helped.

It had nothing to do with him.

As thoughts of running after Kelsie to continue apologizing hit, Marty let it be. Hounding Kelsie to make him like him, wasn't going to work.

Marty read the song selections on the jukebox, and played, '*The Sound of Silence*,' by Simon and Garfunkel.

~

Kelsie poured himself a glass of scotch from a wet bar in the living room. Crystal decanters were placed on a rolling cart, one that seemed to be from the 60s, with etched glasses and a large assortment of libations. He gulped it down, refilled the glass, and took it with him to his room...his private room...and sat down on the bed. He drank more of the scotch, then brought his guitar to his lap. He ran his fingers over the strings and thought about

139

Marty reacting badly to Benjy's help. It was bare minimum assistance, and Kelsie wondered if Marty had been homeless and disconnected from help via a phone, if he would have fared as well.

"You try living on the streets." Kelsie reached for the glass and finished the drink. He felt the heat of the burn down his throat and composed a song in his head.

Chapter 14

Lying on his back on the floor, Marty scrolled through hundreds of TV channels, and nothing interested him. He shut off the set and straightened the room, pushing the beanbags to the side and closing the cabinet under the flat-screen TV. His head low, he walked through the first floor of the house, not hearing Helga or Sigmund, yet, knowing dinner wasn't for a few more hours. Marty explored areas of the home he had not yet seen.

He opened drawers and closets of rooms that seemed to never have been occupied. Nothing was in any of the drawers or closets except linens.

He noticed a wooden door with a latch. Thinking it was another closet, Marty opened it. To his surprise, he found a cellar.

Using the switch on the wall which was covered in paint, as if no one bothered to protect it with tape when the wall was coated, Marty turned on a light. A bulb lit near the bottom of the stairs.

What the heck?

He crept down into the space and the vibe had changed completely from the bright open-plan of the upper floor. The walls were bare concrete with support beams, and it was at that moment that Marty realized the age of this home.

Although it had been upgraded, modernized to appear sleek, the roots and bones of this place told another tale.

Rotted wood, old tools and a workbench, timeworn stools piled seat to seat, their four legs protruding into the dimness like fingers.

The floor was either dirt, or so neglected, the dust had layered.

Spider webs hung from every corner and the smell was of dust and damp.

He opened another wooden door, and turned on the inside light. A wine cellar appeared, complete with its own thermostat and shelves of dusty bottles.

The amount of information Marty knew about wine he could write on his palm. He walked under the low hanging ceiling and wiped the dust from a label. It made him sneeze.

He rubbed his nose and then tried to see a date. When 1809 was written on a bottle label, he became confused. This had to be Benjy's wine cellar. Right?

He rubbed off the grime from centuries of dust to read more dates.

He picked a bottle up and held it to the light to see if it was even palatable. Some sediment was on the bottom, but the wine had been stored on its side, and the thermostat seemed to be working. It was cool here.

Setting the bottle back, imagining asking Helga or Sigmund if they knew about it, Marty continued to explore outside of the wine cellar.

There were so many objects visible in the darkness it felt like he was in an antique shop. A dirty one. The layers of dust were thick.

A shovel and pick axe leaned on one wall, also dusty, and appeared left by a miner.

The floor had become uneven.

Marty kicked at a little lump of dirt and what appeared to be a rock or piece of concrete rolled out of a little indent.

He crouched down to inspect it, thinking it looked curious.

A noise made him startle and he looked at the lit bulb and the stairs. "Kel?"

He kept moving deeper under the house. The area became a maze of rooms, all framed with naked beams and plasterboard, rotting from neglect. Some of the plaster had faded graffiti and drawings, but it was too dark to see what they depicted.

If this cellar was the length of the house, it would be enormous.

There was no natural lighting, no windows, nothing.

Marty ran his fingers over the wall frames, looking for more light switches. He couldn't find anything wired.

"Hello?" he called into the gloom.

Something scurried by, and even though he jumped, he knew it was a mouse.

"Man, this is the stuff of horror movies." Marty rubbed his arms. He kept walking through the maze, his eyes adjusting to the dark, until it became completely black. "Hello?"

Why am I saying that? No one is living down here.

Marty began to retreat and imagined if he needed a diversion, a way to lose himself, this basement was it.

He stood near the racks of bottles and removed one, taking it up the worn wooden stairs and looking over his shoulder as he did. He ended up back in the room he had first explored and could see how dirty his hands were, and his shoes.

He removed the shoes, carrying them out of the room, looking for Kelsie.

~

Kelsie jotted down lyrics he had just made up and thought he heard Marty yelling for him. Since Marty sounded weird, Kelsie set his guitar aside, and poked his head out of his room. "Yeah?"

"Come down!"

Kelsie descended the stairs and found Marty in the kitchen, washing a bottle in the deep stainless steel sink. "What's that?"

"Did you know Benjy had a wine cellar?" He set the bottle on the counter and dried his hands. "Read the date."

143

Kelsie crouched down. "1809?"

"This house has a maze of underground rooms."

"What?" Kelsie tried to read the rest of the label, but it wasn't in English. "Underground?"

"Find a flashlight." Marty began to open cabinets.

"Dude? Why?" He put his hands on his hips. "I'm not really into vintage wine collecting."

"No. No, dude." Marty took a plastic flashlight out of a cleaning supply cabinet. "There's way more. There're old tools, old furniture, and the floor looks as if its dirt."

Kelsie folded his arms. "Still not into it."

"Ghosts?"

"Definitely not into it!" Kelsie held up his hand and backed up.

"Fine." Marty gripped the plastic flashlight and his shoes.

Kelsie watched him walk out of the room. "For real?"

"I have to see what's down there."

"Let me get shoes."

"Okay."

Kelsie raced up the stairs and grabbed socks and his old tennis shoes, then ran back. He sat on the bottom stair and put them on, then nodded for Marty to lead the way.

Marty headed to the farthest room on the lower floor, opposite from where they had set up the home gym.

Kelsie waited for Marty to put his shoes on, then he was astonished to see a wooden door he assumed was a closet. "In there?"

"You're not going to believe this." Marty opened the door, and holding the flashlight, descended a narrow wooden staircase. It was so old, the planks had been worn down in the center of each step.

"Oh, no. This is too creepy." Kelsie crouched to see. Part of the vast space had been made into a wine cellar and was lit by a bare bulb.

Marty turned on the bright flashlight and headed off.

Kelsie was stunned by the immensity of the area. But first, he inspected the wine bottles, all buried under layers of dirt and dust. Only the one spot where the bottle Marty had removed was disturbed.

"Hey." Kelsie looked for him. "Where did you go?"

"I'm here," was called from way off.

Leaving the wine cellar, Kelsie noticed a shovel and pick, and then rusty lanterns, rotted without their glass domes.

He stepped on something and picked it up. "Dude! Is this bone?" He dropped it and rubbed his arms. "Did someone bury someone else down here?"

"I think it's concrete."

"Oh." Kelsie tried to find Marty, but he didn't have a flashlight. "Jesus! What is this place?" He looked into the pitch-darkness in terror. "I can't see you!"

"I'm here!"

Under his breath, Kelsie said, "And I'm not following you."

"Oh, my God! Kelsie! There's an old motorcycle down here!"

"Nope. Nope..." Kelsie wasn't going to budge. He was terrified of being stuck in places like this.

"Dude! Check it out!"

"I don't have a light." Kelsie looked at the wine racks and hoped Helga and Sig could explain to them why it was here.

"Kelsie!"

At Marty's yell, Kelsie froze in fear.

"You have to see this shit!"

Exhaling in relief, Kelsie replied, "Don't do that!"

The patter of Marty's footsteps came closer. Then, Kelsie cold see his light shining in the gloom. "Come here!"

"Do I have to?"

Marty grabbed Kelsie's hand and dragged him through a maze of dark passages.

"Look! This is so weird." Marty shined the light on a cache of secreted items. A motorcycle was barely recognizable in the shadows.

Marty blew on the gas tank, trying to see the markings.

"I don't like this place. You realize now I'm going to have nightmares of being trapped down here."

"Dude. This bike is way old. Look at the seat. That's horsehair. What's painted on the tank? Can you make it out? ACE? Does that say ACE?"

"Nope. I want to get out." Kelsie rubbed his arms.

"Wait. Let me just keep looking. Hold this."

Kelsie took the light.

Marty removed a sheet or blanket from something, and the dust cloud made them both cough and cover their mouths.

A giant clown mask, something that looked like it belonged in a circus or sideshow grinned at them.

Kelsie screamed bloody murder and went to run away.

Marty grabbed hold of Kelsie's shirt. "Calm down!"

"Dude!" Kelsie wanted out.

"Will you stop freaking out?"

Kelsie choked on the dust in the air and tried to hold the light beam on it. "That's so gnarly."

"Benjy had to know about this stuff. It's so him." Marty moved the big clown head and more dirt rained off of it.

"You think I had nightmares before?" Kelsie looked behind him. "No. Uh-uh. We need to have this walled off."

"No way. This stuff may be worth something."

"I can't breathe. I can't. What if someone locks us down here?"

"First of all, no one's home, and Helga isn't going to." Marty dug through boxes. "Wow, this is so dirty. I feel like I'm underground."

"How do you know that wasn't a bone?"

"It had a rock in it." Marty held up a rusty key. "Hmm. Pirate treasure?"

"How can you stand this?" Kelsie kept peering behind him.

Marty left the pile of junk alone and took the flashlight. "Let me just see how far back it goes."

Kelsie clung to Marty, holding his shirt. "Dude. If it spans all the way under the house, I'm not going."

"Hang on." Marty shined the light on either side of them, into cavernous rooms. "I never thought this house had any history. I should have guessed from Benjy's eclectic taste."

"And I was freaked over his Halloween decorations." Kelsie began to feel as if he were inhaling mold. He drew his shirt neck over his mouth and nose.

"He had to have known about this. I mean, he lived here for ages, right?"

"You're asking me?"

Finally, Marty came to a wall. He shone the light over it. It looked as if a tunnel was filled, and a brick archway was visible. "Where did this go?"

"I don't care!" Kelsie tugged on him. "Let's go."

"Now I want to research the history, and the land."

"Go? Now? Please?"

Marty shined the light on all four corners as well as the ceiling. "I guess this is it."

"This is what I imagine hell is like." Something raced across the shadows making Kelsie jump into Marty's arms.

"It's a mouse." Marty pointed the light at the movement.

"Out. Please. Now."

Marty held Kelsie's hand and began to return to the wine cellar. Kelsie spied objects hidden down here, decaying or coated in dust. "This is going to give me horrible nightmares."

"Kel? It's just a basement."

"What if someone's buried down here?"

"Stop watching lousy TV."

They made it back to the cellar with the single hanging bulb.

"I'm going to get that clown mask."

"No!" Kelsie practically climbed on top of him. "It's cursed. Leave it."

"What if it's worth something? And that bike? Come on. That thing may be from World War I."

"Don't mess with this stuff. Bring that bottle back down."

Marty faced him, turning off the flashlight. "Why are you so afraid? Yeah, it's dark, and creepy, but, there's nothing down here."

Kelsie whimpered and made his way up the stairs to escape.

"Take off your shoes!" Marty called after him.

Hopping on one foot, Kelsie did, and then ran all the way back to the kitchen. His legs were covered in dust and cobwebs and his hands were coated with dirt.

~

Marty returned to the clown mask and motorcycle. He looked for some way to identify the bike. The dirt was so caked on it he would have to scrub it off. He could swear he could read an A, and a C. But, he'd never heard of a motorcycle company called ACE.

He thought about asking Sigmund to help him figure it out. Besides, if the only way out was the stairs, he'd never be able to manage removing anything as large as the bike, or the clown mask. *How did they get this stuff down here?*

148

He took a last look around, and then turned off the one bulb and headed up the stairs. He toed off the shoes, seeing how truly filthy he was, including his fingernails.

"Yeck." He shut off the flashlight and found Kelsie curled in a ball in the kitchen, crouching on the floor. Marty set the flashlight back into the cleaning cupboard and put his shoes outside the sliding door, onto the patio.

"I need a shower or bath." He stood beside Kelsie. "Are you okay?"

Kelsie shook his head no.

"Don't worry. I left everything down there."

Kelsie pointed to the bottle. "Not that."

"Kel. If it's turned into vinegar, I'll replace it. But, how cool will it be to drink a vintage bottle of wine?"

"No." Rising up, using the wall behind him, Kelsie shook his head adamantly and scuffed in his socks towards the stairs to the second floor.

"Kelsie?" Marty followed him. "Can you tell me what's really going on?"

"You don't mess with things like that." Kelsie undressed in his room, dropping his dusty clothing to his feet.

Marty did the same, since he was leaving a dusty trail in a spotless home.

Kelsie walked naked into the master bathroom and Marty could hear the water in the shower start.

Marty poked his head into the bathroom. "Did something weird happen to you?"

Kelsie stood under the spray.

Marty watched him. "Not gonna tell me?" When Kelsie crouched in the tub, curled into a ball, Marty grew upset. He stepped into the tub and tried to comfort Kelsie.

But, when his hands got wet, a line of dirt ran down his skin to the bottom of the tub. Marty winced at how filthy he was, and used a sponge to scrub under his nails.

~

Deep in a secret place, Kelsie had hidden, even from himself, odd repressed memories.

That basement was the stuff of his worst nightmares and now that he knew it existed, he had no idea how he was going to stay here.

Marty was busy cleaning off the dirt. Kelsie stared at him, trying to find comfort in the fact that Marty didn't seem afraid. Marty was the one. The brave one.

He handled the scary noises.

He led the way to hunt for an intruder.

Marty, the bank teller, was the real powerhouse of the two.

Kelsie wrapped his arms around Marty's hips and pressed his cheek against Marty's crotch. He closed his eyes and shivered.

"Okay. You're safe. I'll bring the bottle back. Promise."

"Thank you."

"I mean, even if the stuff is worth something, we don't need anything, right?"

"Right."

Marty urged Kelsie to stand, and then used the sponge to wash him off. He took each of Kelsie's hands and made sure they were clean.

Kelsie checked out mentally for a few minutes, allowing Marty to take care of him. It was the first time anyone beside Benjy, had.

~

Phobias were irrational fears. It wasn't up to Marty to diagnose Kelsie's. The basement was eerie, but to Marty, it was like a treasure trove. He couldn't wait to get back down there.

He stood behind Kelsie, using the sponge on his back, washing Kelsie.

Life on the street had obviously made Kelsie nervous and guarded. Although Marty had left home at seventeen, he had never been without a place to sleep or…a job.

Life hadn't been easy for either one of them, but nothing in Marty's life had left him traumatized.

But, he wasn't a psychiatrist. And if Kelsie had phobias or issues, he could only be there for support and not much else.

Kelsie seemed to be snapping out of whatever had gripped him. He shut off the taps and reached for towels, handing one to Marty.

Quietly, they dried off, stepping out of the tub, and rubbing the towels over their hair.

Marty noticed a distant look in Kelsie's green eyes. He draped the towel over the rail and touched Kelsie. "Hey."

Kelsie met his gaze.

Marty took the towel from him and led Kelsie out of the bathroom, to the bedroom. He urged Kelsie under the blanket, and cuddled with him.

Kelsie released a low exhale and intertwined their legs.

He ran his fingers over Kelsie's wet hair, feeling needed, able to give someone comfort and peace.

Kelsie raised his head and they stared at each other.

Then, they met for a kiss.

Marty didn't know what had happened to Kelsie, and maybe he never would, but at that moment, Marty made the decision.

Kelsie O'Loughlin craved exactly what he did, love. It was time he let go of his barriers.

~

Marty's kiss drew Kelsie back to the world of light and love.

Where his nightmares dwelled, and the darkness threatened to take over, Marty represented hope.

151

Kelsie closed his eyes and deepened the kiss. And that kiss, sealed the deal.

He and Marty pressed their naked bodies together, and this time, it meant something; A way to bond, a way to unite, to connect on an intimate level.

It was Marty who made the first contact, as if letting Kelsie know, 'yes'. As Marty reached between them, holding Kelsie's erect cock, Kelsie bent one knee and opened up.

A whimper escaped Marty. With both hands, Marty held Kelsie's length, cupping his balls under it.

Kelsie's respirations elevated to a new height. He parted from the kiss to breathe deeply as Marty massaged the root of his dick, under his balls.

Not wanting to say anything, not wanting to spoil the moment, Kelsie gripped Marty's shoulder, focusing on the pleasure Marty was giving him.

As Marty pressed his lips against Kelsie's neck, nibbling his clean skin, Kelsie felt him squeeze his cock, then a finger rubbed closer to his rim.

"Fuck..." Kelsie bit his lip and went into a climax, one so potent, he held his breath.

~

Feeling Kelsie's cock throb in his palm, his creamy load dripping down his stomach, chills rushed up Marty's spine. He milked Kelsie's cock, prolonging Kelsie's orgasm, the pulsating becoming a slow rhythm. Kelsie brushed against his hand, and wrapped his fingers around Marty's cock. Marty released Kelsie and relaxed as Kelsie reciprocated.

With a similar technique, Kelsie used his spent cum as lube, and drew hand over hand over Marty's erection.

Marty submitted, his arms resting on the bed, and he bent his outer leg. Kelsie cupped his balls and manipulated them gently, then ran his sticky fingers behind them, to the base of his cock.

Marty drew in a deep breath and clenched his fists.

Kelsie rubbed vigorously between Marty's legs and then against his rim.

Marty's body jerked involuntarily as he came, his toes spreading and curling. He felt the warm spatter against his skin, and drifted off on the waves of bliss.

Kelsie slowed his motion, and then, released Marty's cock.

They embraced, kissing each other's cheek and neck, making soft sounds of affection.

Chapter 15

After cuddling and giggling like teens, they climbed out of bed and got dressed.

Kelsie led the way down the stairs. He could smell something cooking and his stomach grumbled.

Just as he and Marty entered the dining room, seeing the table once more set, Helga brought out the wine Marty had found. It was decanting in a crystal bottle, and two stemmed glasses were beside it.

She set the tray down and poured for them.

Marty asked, "Did you know there was a wine cellar, Helga?"

"Wait." Kelsie stopped them. "I thought we were putting that back."

"I did know." Helga handed Marty the glass. "Benjy didn't like wine."

"What?" Marty blinked in surprise and then sniffed the wine. "Is it still good? Or vinegar?"

Kelsie shook his head, not wanting to mess around with anything supernatural.

"I assure you, the wine cellar is climate controlled."

Marty sipped the dark red wine. "Oh, man, that's smooth. Pour yourself and Sigmund a glass, Helga. Please."

"That's very kind." She smiled.

"Kel." Marty drank more. "You gotta try this."

"I thought..." He watched Helga fill two glasses, and, Sigmund, wearing an apron, his shaven head shining in the sunlight, raised a glass for a toast. "To Benjy."

"To Benjy." Marty held his up.

Kelsie began to feel outnumbered, and a little silly. He held up the glass and all four of them tapped it in a toast to their late friend.

"Mm." Sigmund showed his approval. "Superb."

"It's like velvet. Taste it, Kelsie." Marty finished his.

Kelsie sniffed it. It had an oak-fruity scent. He wasn't a wine connoisseur, to say the least. He sipped it, thought it tasted like any other red wine he'd had to drink, and set the glass down. "Can I have a sweet cocktail?"

Helga winked at him. "Of course." She returned to the kitchen.

"Sig?" Marty followed the chef into the kitchen. "What do you know about the stuff left in the basement?"

Kelsie shivered in a chill even though he knew his fears were unfounded. He walked to the sliding glass doors, and opened them, yearning the sunshine and warmth. Anything was better than the creepy cellar.

He stood by the pool and inhaled deeply, then thought about his and Marty's mutual hand-jobs and shook off the irrational fear of enjoying wine coming from a dusty cellar.

~

Marty had a peek at the chicken marinating for dinner. It appeared either a barbeque was planned, or they were going to use the kitchen grill, which was part of the island counter, and included a hood for the exhaust.

"Did you know there's a motorcycle down there?" Marty set his glass on the counter.

"I do recall something about it. I believe Benjy's grandfather may have left a few items."

"Should we try to get the stuff out? Let them see daylight?" Marty asked as Helga began to create a fruity cocktail.

"That's up to you and Kelsie now." Sigmund sipped the wine, then he began to slice vegetables for a salad.

"How would we get a motorcycle out of there?"

Helga tried to time her use of the blender so she didn't make a racket while he spoke.

Once she whizzed the concoction, Sigmund replied, "We could make a ramp on the stairs and simply roll the bike out."

"I think the gas tank said, A-C-E. Can that be right? I should look it up on the computer." Marty watched Helga slice fruit for Kelsie's cocktail. "Man, that looks refreshing."

She smiled knowingly, and took a second glass from the cabinet.

"I mean, I like wine, but I love your cocktails." Marty laughed shyly.

After she added a swizzle stick with pineapple and mango, she handed it to him. "There ya go."

"Thanks!" Marty watched her bring Kelsie the second glass and focused on Sigmund. He was a middle-aged man, tall and sturdy. "So, I can do what I want with the stuff in the basement?"

"It's your home now. Yours and Kelsie's. You can certainly do as you please." Sigmund cut grilled corn off the cob. It was slightly charred and looked delicious."

Marty sipped the sweet cocktail and licked his lips. "You don't know of any funny business that happened down there, right?"

Sigmund appeared to try to hide his hilarity. "You did know Benjy, correct?"

"Ha." Marty stirred the drink with the fruit-swizzle stick. "I mean, nasty business…wait. Let me rephrase that."

Sigmund chuckled. "Do you mean something violent or tragic?"

"Yes." Marty pointed to him. "Like that."

Sigmund wiped his hands on a towel. "Well...not to my knowledge. This home is over a hundred years old. You'd have to consult a historian or some other reference."

"Okay." Marty figured as much. The only thing scary down in the cellar, were rodents.

~

Kelsie sat on the pool ledge, his feet in the water, kicking gently. He was buzzed on the sweet cocktail and ruminated about the progress he and Marty had made in bed.

Hearing the slider open, Kelsie glanced back to see Marty with his small laptop computer. He sat beside Kelsie and read the screen.

"I know I seem superstitious."

Marty looked up from the computer.

Kelsie stared at his feet in the pool water. "I had a fucked up childhood."

Marty gave him his undivided attention.

"My...my grandmother said I was cursed." Kelsie squinted into the sunlight. "They used to bring me to a pastor..." Kelsie cleared his throat. "He...he locked me in a dark room."

"Geez." Marty shook his head.

"Then..." Kelsie sighed. "Never mind." He leaned back so he could see the laptop. "What are you looking up?"

"That motorcycle. There's a motorcycle company called Ace. I think that bike may be a 1920s or something. Forget it. You were saying?"

"Did Sig know anything about the stuff down there?"

"Not really." Marty set the laptop aside. "Do you want to talk about it?"

"I just don't want you to think I'm a lunatic or something." Leaning back, Kelsie rested his weight on his hands. "It's just some emotional baggage shit. I know it's crazy."

"No. It's not crazy. You're not crazy."

Kelsie brushed off his hands and drew his feet out of the water. "It's just...being confined in dark, scary places." He shivered in exaggeration. "I can't. I get really messed up."

"It's okay."

"Not really. Now that I know that cellar exists, I'm going to have nightmares."

"Kel."

He turned to look at Marty.

"I'm here. I won't ever let you get trapped down there. I mean, you can't. We'll take off the lock if—"

"No. Keep the lock. I want to be able to stop what's down there from coming into the house."

"Nothing is down there." Marty put his arm around him.

"I thought I'd be the tough guy." Kelsie dabbed at the corner of his eye.

"You are tough. I wouldn't last one day on the street."

Kelsie rested his head on Marty's shoulder and released a deep sigh. "I never even told Benjy."

"You could have. He would have been there for you."

"I think he knew I'd been through some shit." Kelsie sniffled. "I didn't have to spell it out."

"That's another thing I adored about Benjy. He seemed to get me too. And, I didn't have to tell him how insecure I felt. He knew."

Kelsie put his arm around Marty. "Fuck, I miss him."

"Me too."

They both perked up as the sliding door opened. Sigmund held a platter of marinated chicken, then set it down, and started the gas barbeque heating.

"Mm." Marty smiled at Kelsie. "Barbecued chicken."

"Yum." Kelsie rested his head on Marty's shoulder again.

~

THE ODD COUPLE

Kelsie licked the sauce off his fingers, and was buzzed on the sweet mango-pineapple cocktails. Even though he was stuffed, he took another helping of the roasted corn salad.

Marty had given up, patting his belly and moaning.

"How was it?" Helga asked, clearing plates.

"Too good." Marty drank ice water.

Kelsie stuffed the last bite of corn into his mouth and chewed, then handed his plate to her. "I think I'm going to explode."

"Any room for dessert?"

Both he and Marty said, "No," at the same time.

"I need to walk this off." Marty held his belly.

"We could." Kelsie wiped his mouth with the cloth napkin.

"On the treadmill?"

"No. Walk. Like in, outdoors. On our street."

"Oh." Marty stacked a few plates as Kelsie stood, waiting for him. "Thanks, Helga and Sig!"

"You're welcome!"

Kelsie gestured for Marty to go first. "I sort of need to get out of this house. I feel as though we've been in here since we moved in."

"I went to work...well, for a few minutes at least. And we hit the ATM and beach."

"You know what I mean." Kelsie headed up the stairs, holding the rail.

They split off when they made it to the top landing, going to their bedrooms.

Kelsie changed out of his shorts and into jeans, putting on a decent shirt, one he'd found in the closet belonging to Benjy. He didn't have much of a wardrobe selection himself.

He checked the brightly-printed top in the full-length mirror and patted his full stomach.

Once he finished changing, Kelsie looked at his phone. No messages.

159

"Why do I even have this?" He shook his head and left it where it was. Putting on socks and sneakers, Kelsie headed to Marty's room.

Marty had done the same, changing into jeans and a denim shirt since the evenings were cool from the wind. They gave each other a nod that they were ready, and Kelsie headed to the front door. "Do we need a key?"

"I've got one. Helga and Sigmund usually leave after dinner." Marty showed Kelsie his key.

Kelsie walked outside and stared at his and Marty's cars, which were still where they had left them. He pointed them out. "We either need to get rid of them, or hide them in the garage."

"You're right. They don't look very good here." Marty reached out his hand, and Kelsie clasped it.

They walked down the long driveway to the street, using a small gate to exit, closing it behind them. There were no sidewalks but the traffic lane was relatively wide.

"Which way?" Marty asked.

"Up." He pointed to the incline in the lane.

As they walked along the road, Kelsie interlaced their fingers. It occurred to him he had never been in public holding a man's hand before. He indicated it, and said, "Do you think someone will deliberately aim for us?"

"No." Marty smiled, as if Kelsie were joking. "I'm glad you suggested this. I need to stop eating so much."

"It's tough. The food is too good. And I'm used to starving."

Marty squeezed his fingers. "Starving?"

Kelsie lowered his head and avoided stepping on old road-kill, then evaded the topic. "So...this is it, huh?"

"Are you complaining?"

"No. I'm happy, I guess." Kelsie caught glimpses of the view behind the hedges, high fences, and mansions.

"It's funny, huh? How when we're in a lousy place, we're unhappy, and here we are, like two lottery winners, still wondering if we're happy."

Swinging their arms as they walked, Kelsie thought about that truth. "It's a big change. I guess it's going to take time. I mean, we just fell into this unexpectedly."

"You have to admit, it's working out better than you imagined." Marty held up their hands. "We don't hate each other."

Kelsie smiled. "No. I don't hate you."

After a few moments of quiet contemplation, they came upon a grassy patch of land with a view. Both of them were drawn to it, and stood to look out at the distant hills.

Kelsie put his arm around Marty instead of holding his hand. "Do you think you could ever love me?"

Marty reciprocated, holding him as well, squeezing Kelsie closer, answering his question without a word.

~

As Marty stood on the lookout point, holding onto a man, one he would never have guessed would be his friend, let alone his lover, he thought about what a difference a few days had made.

He'd gone from a lonely, insecure, bank teller, to someone's boyfriend and hero.

At first he had questioned Benjy's judgment; sticking them together, a pair of unlikely matched men. But, Benjy had proven to be the wise man he had always admired.

The only thing that would have been better was if Benjy hadn't passed away.

As he withstood the wind and stared at the distant hills, Marty knew, if Benjy hadn't died, he wouldn't be with a potential life partner and have shed his insecure skin. He wondered why Benjy hadn't introduced him to Kelsie before.

But, as he thought more about it, he realized why.

Benjy had enjoyed sex with Kelsie.

He faced Kelsie, holding his waist, and they stared into each other's eyes. "Am I sleeping in your room tonight?"

"I don't care which room, as long as we're together."

Marty leaned in for a kiss.

As they smooched, a car horn beeped, startling them.

When Marty looked, he could see the driver smiling and pumping his fist in support.

It had made Kelsie chuckle. "That's better than running us over or flipping us off."

"Yes. It is." Marty looked out at the horizon and smiled.

~

They spent a little over an hour walking, exploring the neighborhood, seeing mansions, manicured lawns and gated driveways.

As evening drew closer, and the wind became colder, they returned to their home.

Kelsie waited for Marty to turn the key, and they entered the foyer. The house was empty now that the couple had gone home. Marty headed up the stairs, leaving Kelsie to do his own thing.

He removed his shoes, stopped to relieve himself and wash his hands, then made his way to his favorite room. He turned on the lights in the game-room and stood at the jukebox.

Before he made his selection, he heard Marty whisper, "Come to bed."

Kelsie turned to look. Marty was there, reaching out his hand.

Knowing this was an invitation to bond intimately, Kelsie left the music silent and joined Marty on his return to their bedroom.

Marty said, "You left rubbers and lube on my nightstand."

"I did." Kelsie shook his head at himself.

"I guess we'll use them. Right?"

"Right." He entered Marty's bedroom and watched as Marty turned down the bed and finished undressing.

Kelsie became nervous. This time, it was going to mean something. It was going to matter.

~

This was how Marty had imagined it.

The lights low, the twilight glowing pink and peach outside, and romance in the air.

Kelsie dropped his clothing to the floor at the foot of the bed, and climbed on the mattress.

Marty had already set out what they would need for lovemaking, and relaxed on his back, his head on a pillow.

Kelsie lay beside him, staring at him with luminous green eyes.

Facing him, cupping Kelsie's jaw over his beard growth, Marty went for a kiss. While anticipating Kelsie would go crazy and pin him to the bed, Marty was pleasantly surprised. Kelsie was willing to savor the moment.

The kissing heated up and they both held each other's face, swirling their tongues and getting excited.

Marty reached between them, righting both of their cocks and gently smoothing his hand over Kelsie's. Kelsie made a soft sound against his mouth and bent his leg.

Marty parted from the kiss, gazing at Kelsie, seeing his patient expression. He rolled to his back, straddled his legs and urged Kelsie on top of him.

Kelsie kissed his way across Marty's chest, and made himself comfortable between Marty's legs.

They continued the sexy kissing, Marty digging his fingers into Kelsie's hair as Kelsie propped himself up on his forearms.

Marty reached between them again and pointed Kelsie's cock at his rim. He was ready. This was exactly as he imagined it.

Kelsie parted from the kiss and reached for the condoms.

Marty caressed Kelsie's nipples to keep him excited as Kelsie rolled on the rubber. Once Kelsie was ready and had spread lubrication on his sheathed cock, Marty held his own knees, pulling them back, and invited Kelsie in.

~

His nervousness had vanished.

Marty was teaching him the art of real lovemaking. And Kelsie was eating it up.

He used the head of his cock to massage between Marty's legs, then pressed it against Marty's rim. As the head of his cock began to penetrate Marty's body, Kelsie glanced at Marty's face. "Okay?"

"Yes." Marty gave him a fabulous smile.

The expression of affection and trust was more exciting than the physical pleasure. This was bonding, bringing them closer than they ever were, and it made a difference.

Kelsie held Marty's legs and began a slow rhythm, allowing Marty to relax and take some of the control. They let it build, not hammering for the climax-fix, like Kelsie had done previously.

When Marty touched himself, pulling on his erection, Kelsie felt a shiver of chills at the sight. He licked his lips and encouraged Marty to please himself while getting fucked.

"Still okay?" Kelsie was as deep as he desired.

"Yes." Marty held onto his cock and whimpered sensually.

This time, Kelsie was going to savor pleasing Marty, before he came.

~

The internal friction was setting him on fire. Marty rose to a climax and the fact that Kelsie was being considerate and giving him a chance to enjoy it was a bonus.

A wash of intense pleasure hit Marty's groin and he came. He closed his eyes and squeezed his dick, feeling the warm spatter of his cum.

"Oh, fuck yeah." Kelsie seemed to get off on it as much as Marty was. He thrust faster and the searing heat whipped through Marty.

Marty gasped and released his hold on his cock, spreading out his arms and enjoying the pulsating rushes.

Kelsie pushed in as deeply as he could, and Marty felt Kelsie's climax as their two bodies throbbed against each other.

Kelsie caught his breath and pulled out, sitting on his heels, releasing Marty's legs to allow him to straighten them.

He stared at the full tip of the condom and caught his breath. "That was awesome."

"Yes. It was."

Kelsie moved higher on the bed and kissed Marty. "Thank you for being patient and not rejecting me."

"My pleasure." Marty gave him a silly smile.

Kelsie kissed him again and rolled off the bed, holding out his hand.

They entered the bathroom to wash up, stealing glances at each other as they did.

~

After the amazing sex, he and Marty sprawled out on the floor in the game room, watching TV. It was a Monday night and a few decent shows were on the premium channels.

Kelsie began to doze off as the show ended. He rubbed his face, yawning. "Do you want to go to sleep?"

"It's only ten." Marty pointed the remote at the TV to view the menu.

"Why am I so tired?" Kelsie snuggled beside him, one arm around Marty's back. He watched Marty scroll through the selections. "No news channels, please."

"Agreed."

Kelsie rolled to his back and stared at the ceiling light fixture. It was also 'vintage' with brass fittings and frosted glass. "Why didn't Benjy leave this estate to Sig and Helga?"

"I have no idea. I imagine they get paid well." Marty kept the remote control pointed at the TV.

"They don't seem angry or resentful." Kelsie looked at his nails.

"Nope. They don't."

"It must be sort of nice working with your spouse at a job you like."

"They do seem pretty content. I would imagine we'd sense something if they weren't."

"They'd poison our food." When Kelsie didn't hear an answer, he took a look at Marty. "What?"

"You're more paranoid than I am." Marty turned off the TV set.

"I have trust issues."

"Ya think?" Marty snuggled.

"I trust you." Kelsie urged Marty to lie on top of him.

"I'm flattered." Marty leaned on his elbow and stared at him.

"Did you lock that door to the basement?"

"Really?" Marty appeared surprised.

Kelsie cleared his throat. "You did, right?"

"I think so."

"You think so?"

"I'll check." Marty made a move to stand.

"No."

"How can I check on it if I can't stand up?"

Kelsie released him and watched him leave the room. He shouted, "You're fearless!" At the thought of walking through this empty house and going anywhere near that door, Kelsie shivered and shook his head. "Why did he ever tell me about it?"

~

THE ODD COUPLE

Marty made his way through the quiet home, hoping Kelsie would get over his phobia. It was a basement, that's all.

He entered the room where the door was, and noticed not only was it not locked, it was ajar.

Marty opened the door and looked down the rutty stairs. He turned on the light and listened. Nope. Nothing.

He turned off the light and closed the door, moving the latch, when he noticed something floating from the gust of shutting the door.

Marty held out his palm and a tiny red feather landed on it.

He looked up, and then around. "Nice one, Benjy." He trapped it and took a last peek at the room, then closed the door to it as well.

When he returned to the game room, Kelsie was still lying on the floor, waiting.

"Benjy says, don't worry." Marty smiled.

"Huh?" Kelsie sat up, then made it to his feet.

Marty opened his hand and showed him the tiny feather.

"What's that?"

"Obviously it's a feather. It looks like it's from one of Benjy's boas." Marty held it in his fingers, studying it.

Kelsie crossed his arms. "So? Nothing weird? The door was locked?"

"No. It wasn't locked. I locked it." He turned off the light in the room. "Bedtime?" Marty headed up the stairs making sure the lights were off and the front door was bolted.

"What do you mean, you locked it?" Kelsie climbed the stairs behind him.

"Will you chill? Helga or Sigmund may have gone down there after we mentioned it." He paused at the top landing. "You're sleeping in my room, right?"

"Hell yeah!" Kelsie appeared panicked.

Marty handed him the feather. "Our buddy is here watching over us." He set the feather in Kelsie's palm. "See ya after you wash up." Marty walked to his room.

~

Kelsie cupped the little feather and stepped into the master bedroom suite. He turned on a light and shivered. "Ya here, Benjy?"

Kelsie set the little feather on the dresser near his phone, and it blew off the top in an invisible breeze.

"Why am I so freaked out?" He rubbed his arms. He told himself, "Dude. Chill." He got ready for bed in the bathroom and tried to shake off the nerves.

He washed his face and brushed his teeth, then focused on getting ready for sleep, *with* Marty.

Kelsie took off his clothing and opened the walk-in closet. He picked out a pair of Benjy's pajama bottoms, one with wild animal-print patterns on them. He put them on and was about to go to Marty's room when he remembered Benjy wearing these particular pants.

Dahhhling! I was so in love! We loved and loved and loved! Then? Nothing. No sex. I found out he was married...and a politician!

Kelsie chuckled to himself and touched the soft fabric. "Thanks, Benjy. I needed that."

~

Marty turned down the bed and checked his phone. No messages. "Whatever."

He slapped it down on the dresser, and shut off the overhead light, turning on the table lamp. Before he climbed into bed, he listened for Kelsie.

168

Since it felt like a long time, and he knew Kelsie was anxious, he walked down the hallway and peeked into Kelsie's room. He was on his hands and knees, crawling on the floor.

"Did you lose something?"

"That feather."

Marty blinked in confusion. "Um, you have a closet full of feather boas."

"No. That one was a sign." He ran his fingers over the white carpet.

Marty inspected the billowy pajama bottoms Kelsie had on, then looked at his own. They were both dressed in Benjy's jammies.

"Got it." Kelsie held it up.

"Are you that superstitious?"

"It was a sign." Kelsie approached him. "Where can I keep it?"

"Um..." Marty shrugged. "I'm going to bed."

"Hang on."

Marty paused at the doorway and watched Kelsie carefully put the little feather into a wooden box on the dresser top. After he made sure it had indeed gone into the little box, Kelsie exhaled. "Okay."

"And I thought I had OCD." Marty waved him over.

Kelsie walked with him. "You're the one who said it was from him."

"I was joking." Marty waited for Kelsie to enter the room, then he closed the door.

"Is there a lock?" Kelsie asked as he sat on the bed.

Marty turned the latch on the doorknob. "Okay?"

"Okay."

He and Kelsie snuggled in the bed and Marty turned off the light. He felt Kelsie's legs intertwine with his own under the sheet. "No nightmares."

"I can't promise anything." Kelsie pulled him close.

"No getting scared of the house-settling noise either."

"You sure demand a lot."

"I just want to feel safe. If you keep scaring me, we're going to struggle to live here." Marty put his arm around Kelsie.

"You're right. I'm sorry. Benjy won't let anything happen to us."

"Exactly. He never would."

"Goodnight."

"Goodnight, Kel."

~

It's no problem at all, Kel...just let me remove anything valuable from there, and I'll wall it up. You won't even know a door was there.

Thanks, Benjy. I mean it. Your basement scares me.

That's just silly. All right. Let me tell Helga and Sig to take the wine, since no one else seems to like it.

I think they'd appreciate that, Benjy.

It isn't like I haven't given them anything.

I know. You're the best.

Sweet dreams, Kel.

Kelsie smiled and curled into the cottony bedding, floating in his dream.

~

Marty opened his eyes in the dark room. He peeked at the digital clock and it read three a.m. He heard Kelsie giggle.

He had a look at him in the dimness, and Kelsie appeared to be sleeping soundly. Just as he was about to roll over and disregard the distraction, Kelsie spoke in his sleep.

"Thanks, Benjy."

Marty leaned up on his elbow and stared at Kelsie. Seeing him smile, Marty wondered what the dream was about. But, as long as it wasn't scary, he was thankful. He nestled around Kelsie and liked sleeping with him. He may not be as terrified as Kelsie was about the big house, but it was nice to share a bed with someone you liked...a lot.

He held Kelsie close and fell back asleep.

Chapter 16

Kelsie began to come around from a sound sleep. He rolled to his back, stretched his legs and curled his toes.

A big, clean comfy bed. It was the little things in life you miss.

He shifted to his side and smiled at Marty, who was still sleeping. Kelsie touched his own morning erection through the cotton pants and imagined fooling around.

As he considered waking Marty with a kiss to his cheek, Kelsie heard noises coming from the floor below. It was normal for Sigmund and Helga to arrive early to get their breakfast ready and prepare for the day.

Kelsie tucked his hand into his pants and held his dick as he imagined he and Marty exchanging hand-jobs.

Then, another noise caught his attention. Caught between his idle curiosity and being horny, Kelsie became distracted. Then, the sound of talking in the foyer became audible.

Curiosity won.

He sat up and pushed at his dick to calm down. Walking to the door, he turned the handle which unlocked it, and pulled it open. Yup. Sigmund was definitely talking to someone.

Kelsie stood at the top landing, looking over the rail.

A man carried a cardboard box out of the house.

When he spotted Sigmund, Kelsie called to him, "Sig?"

The older man looked up at him. "Yes?"

"Who's that guy?"

"He's taking the most of the wine, as you requested."

"Oh." Kelsie nodded, and then did a double-take. "As I requested?"

Sigmund walked closer to the stairs. "You instructed for the basement to be emptied of valuables and sealed up, right?"

A strange feeling of disorientation gripped him. Trying to figure out if he had, or if it was a dream, Kelsie touched his lip.

"Kel?"

He started at Marty standing behind him.

"What's going on?" Marty had a look over the rail.

"Sir?" Sigmund seemed to be checking if his actions were correct.

"Yes." Kelsie didn't care how he knew, but getting that space cleared and plastered over was essential.

Sigmund continued his task.

"Kelsie?" Marty yawned and rubbed his face. "What did I miss?"

Kelsie headed to his bedroom to wash up in his private bathroom. He was confused and trying to sort out his thoughts.

~

Marty spotted men coming into the house. He put on a robe and headed down the stairs. As he investigated, he was surprised to see the men had built a ramp to the basement and were carting out the wine, as well as bringing up anything that could have value, from the cellar.

He heard knocking on the walls, and then they wheeled the old motorcycle up while Sigmund made sure the floors were covered to keep them clean.

"You got it up here. Wow." Marty wrapped the robe closer around him and took a look at the dust-covered bike.

"I think it's best to place it in an auction."

"Absolutely." Marty nodded. "The wine as well?"

"Yes."

"Thanks. I'm really glad you took the initiative to do this."

Sigmund stared at Marty for a moment, then said, "It was at Kelsie's request."

Marty heard the men heading back down the stairs and then they emerged with the clown. "See? Nothing scary about it."

"I agree."

"Thanks, Sig." Marty returned to the staircase to find out what Kelsie wanted to do about working out. He stood in the master suite bathroom as Kelsie showered. "Hey."

Kelsie held his chest.

"Sorry." Marty smiled. "I guess we're not working out?"

"Oh. I completely forgot." Kelsie rinsed the shampoo.

Marty leaned on the wall as he watched him. "Thanks for letting Sigmund auction that stuff."

Kelsie shot him a worried look, then shut off the taps. "Ya know, Marty, I can't recall telling him to do that."

Marty shrugged. "Sig is really cool. He probably figured it out." Marty backed up as Kelsie stepped out of the shower and wrapped a towel around himself.

"Did we tell him?" Kelsie bit his lip.

"Maybe not directly."

"Dude." Kelsie rubbed the towel over his hair. "Either he's a clairvoyant or I'm losing my mind."

"Kel." Marty chided him, "Stop over-thinking shit. You sound like me." He was about to head to his own room when Kelsie stopped him.

"No. Marty. Listen. I had a dream about Benjy last night."

"I know. I heard you talking and giggling in your sleep."

Kelsie's eyes widened. "Really?"

"Yes."

"What did I say?" He wrapped the towel around his hips.

"I can't recall exactly. Let me clean up if we're not working out." Marty thought about the exercise room and shrugged. It wasn't as if it was going anywhere.

THE ODD COUPLE

~

Kelsie stared at his reflection in the mirror over the sink and struggled to think. "I must have told him. He saw how I reacted to the wine." He waved at his own reflection dismissively and finished getting dressed.

Kelsie met Marty at the top landing and they both headed down the staircase as more items were being removed from the basement. Kelsie paused to look at the truck parked out in front. Seeing his car was in the way, he trotted up the stairs and grabbed his key, and his shoes, and raced back down.

"Sorry!" Kelsie said as he avoided the men. He sat in his car, and drove around the curved driveway to the garage. He parked in front of the garage door, and when it rolled up on its own, he was surprised, until he saw Marty holding the remote opener.

Kelsie waved at him in thanks, and parked next to the cars already inside it. As he climbed out, he spotted Marty doing the same.

With their cars in the detached garage, it was now full.

Marty exited his car, walking out of the garage with Kelsie, and then closing the doors again.

"Why do I keep feeling like a pain in the ass?" Kelsie returned to the house with Marty.

"Hey. We just moved in. We'll get there."

They waited until the two movers cleared the doorway, and made their way to the kitchen.

Helga smiled at their approach and poured coffee for them. "What are you two hungry for?"

"Your wonderful breakfast," Marty said, taking his usual seat.

While she poured coffee for them, Kelsie asked, "Should we donate whatever we make on those items to Benjy's favorite charities?"

175

Marty said, "Yes!" quickly, and then poured cream into his cup.

"That's a very generous thought, Kelsie." Helga patted his shoulder. "You two are wonderful young men."

"It would make Benjy proud." Marty held his cup in his hands.

"Helga?" Kelsie asked before she entered the kitchen.

"Yes?"

"How did you guys know to remove that stuff and wall up the cellar?"

"Wall it up?" Marty blinked.

"Don't you recall telling us?" Helga asked.

Kelsie began to wonder about his sanity. "Never mind."

"How about I make you two a wonderful garden vegetable omelet?"

"With cheese?" Marty asked.

"With cheese." Helga gave him a sweet smile.

Kelsie waited for her to go into the kitchen, then he said, "I don't remember telling them to do that."

"Don't sweat it. They saw how you reacted to the wine bottle." Marty glanced at the newspapers that were folded on the table.

Both he and Kelsie turned to look as other items were being removed from the cellar.

"You won't be comfortable until we actually wall that place up?" Marty spoke softly. "There's a working wine cellar down there."

"Do you want old wine?"

"No. But...it does seem extreme."

Kelsie didn't think it was. And, he had a memory of Benjy letting him know it was fine with him.

As he thought about that recollection, he realized he couldn't possibly have discussed it with Benjy since Kelsie didn't even know it was there until yesterday. "Huh."

"What?"

"That dream? I think Benjy visited me. I swear, he told me he was going to deal with it."

"The dream was more wishful thinking than a real dream."

"Do you believe in life after death?" Kelsie drank the coffee down quickly, craving more.

"I'm not sure but, I believe in death after life. Do you think Benjy's still here?"

"He loved this place. I would stay if I were him." Kelsie looked up when Sigmund approached the table. He had something cupped into his hands.

"What did you find?" Marty perked up.

"Old coins. I doubt they're worth anything, but the dates are intriguing." Sigmund gestured to the kitchen. "Let me clean them up."

"Cool." Marty smiled.

Kelsie felt a nervous twinge in his gut. "Well, we disturbed everything that was down there. If we're going to get haunted, it's too late now."

"If it's Benjy's ghost, I want him here."

Kelsie had no idea who had lived or died in this home, but he wasn't keen on the idea of having anything going 'bump' in the night.

Helga brought two plates of food to them.

Marty sat up and held his knife and fork ready.

Kelsie inhaled the roasted potatoes and onions, and his mouth watered at the sight of the melted cheese on the omelet. "Wow."

Once she topped up their coffee cups, Helga said, "Enjoy."

Sigmund held out the coins he'd found.

Kelsie didn't want anything to do with them, while Marty eagerly took them to inspect.

"Look at the dates. They're so cool, Sig." Marty held each up. "Do you collect coins?"

"I don't. My nephew does."

"Kelsie? Do you want them?" Marty asked.

"Nope." He chewed on the omelet, shoveling it into his mouth.

"They're all yours." Marty handed them back to Sigmund.

"I'll let you know if we find anything else." Sigmund cupped the few coins into his hand.

"No bodies, please." Kelsie shivered.

Sigmund shook his head at the comment, obviously thinking it was a joke.

Marty waited for Sigmund to leave, and whispered, "You really need to quit the spooky talk. The last thing I want to find in this place is a body or a hundred-year-old murder mystery."

"Should have never gone down there." Kelsie chewed on the sautéed mushrooms and peppers.

"Well, like you wanted, it's going to be walled up and forgotten."

"Good." Kelsie sipped more coffee, trying to figure out how he had let Sigmund know he wanted the basement erased.

~

After breakfast, Marty investigated the little excavation going on in the cellar. Sigmund had hired a crew of men to disconnect the temperature controlled unit of the wine cellar.

He headed down the ramp and noticed spotlights had been strung up to help them see what they were doing. Marty had a look through a pile of rusty items, seeing most of the value had been stolen by decay and time.

Even though he knew it was silly, he looked at the floor, trying to detect if anything appeared to be disturbed or buried.

With the aid of bright lights, Marty couldn't find anything that appeared odd. He heard murmuring and shuffling. Marty walked towards the farthest space, seeing the men making sure nothing was left behind.

They paused in their work and glanced at him.

Marty pointed to the stone archway. "What do you think that is?"

One of the men wearing a baseball cap and gloves, replied, "I think it was a cold storage, before refrigeration."

Nodding, Marty said, "That makes sense."

"Do you want to get a pest control company down here?"

"How bad is the mouse infestation?" Marty tried to see if there were holes or droppings.

"Not too bad. But, it may be a good idea so they don't move into the house."

"Then, absolutely."

"It will delay us plastering over the door."

Marty was undecided about sealing this area up. It was history, not fear, that drove him. "Exterminator first, wall it up, last."

"Okay." The man took out his phone and then said, "No service down here."

Another man said, "It's the concrete walls."

The first man walked by Marty to the stairs.

Marty had a look around the perimeter. "So, in your opinion, anything down here appear to have been used for a crime?"

"Maybe bootlegging." He shrugged. "No way to know unless you start digging...or use some kind of ultrasound to see under the dirt."

"Nope." Marty shook his head. "Let sleeping dogs lie."

"Is there any reason to think something happened here?"

"No. Only irrational fear of cellars." Marty laughed.

"Well, that clown was fucked up." He chuckled.

"I'm probably the only one who thought it was cool."

"Do you live here?" The man shifted his stance and removed his gloves.

"Yes. I do, with my friend Kelsie."

"What do you do for a living? If you don't mind me asking."

Before he said he was a bank teller, he took a moment to think about what the man was actually asking.

The first man returned, walking down the ramp. "They're coming in a few hours. We can't find anything else here to salvage."

"Okay." Marty assumed they had cleared out what they could. "Thanks."

They shut off the spotlights, leaving them for the exterminator. Marty returned to the stairs/ramp and held the railing as he climbed up. Sigmund had the floors covered up to avoid a mess, but still, Marty removed his shoes.

Once they were all on the same level, Marty shut the door and latched it, because he knew Kelsie would be upset if he didn't. He watched the first man leave the room, and then looked at the second man, the one who had asked him the question. "This home was left to me and my friend in a will."

The man appeared surprised. "Wow. That's amazing."

"Yeah. It really is." Marty walked with the man to the front door. "But, I'd rather have him, than the house."

He got a sad smile from the man, and then Marty climbed the stairs to wash up.

~

Kelsie sat on the edge of the pool, his feet in the water, soaking up the sun. He felt a tickling on his shoulder, and brushed at it, assuming it was a bug.

A tiny red feather floated, rocking side to side, and landed on his leg.

Kelsie stared at it curiously and looked upwards, squinting in the brightness. "Benjy?"

The sliding door opened and Kelsie held his chest from the start. "Man. I have got to stop being so jumpy."

Marty emerged from the house and sat beside him.

"Look." Kelsie held up the little feather.

"You're carrying it around with you?"

"This just fell on me."

"From where?"

He and Marty scanned the eaves and trees. Marty sank his feet into the water and kicked gently. "We decided to deal with the mice and then, well...decide if we should seal it up."

Kelsie held the little feather in his fingers to inspect. "Do you think he's here?"

"Who? Benjy?"

"Yeah. What's with the feathers?"

"You wore the boa in the kitchen. Maybe it just stuck to your feet or something."

"Should we do a séance?" When he didn't hear an answer, he looked at Marty. "Marty?"

"I don't know. I'm not sure I believe in them."

Kelsie tried to set the feather aside, but it floated on the invisible breeze, vanishing. "He's here. I know he's here."

"I'm okay with that. It's his house."

"Were there any bones in the basement?"

"No."

"Phew."

Marty nudged Kelsie with his shoulder and shook his head.

Chapter 17

Kelsie wandered to the room with the basement door, strangely drawn to it.

He could hear men working below, the exterminators had come.

Kelsie stepped over the drop-cloths that Sigmund had laid out, and stood near a window, which faced the back of the property. With his hands in his shorts' pockets, he gazed at the shrubs that were planted near the house, and thought about trying to contact Benjy via a psychic medium or an Ouija board.

As workers came and went from the cellar, Kelsie started to believe his fear of the dark was indeed, irrational. Just because he had been neglected as a kid, didn't mean anything sinister was residing here.

When he spotted Sigmund checking on the progress, Kelsie got his attention. "Sig?"

"Yes?" The older man approached him.

"Do you believe in ghosts?"

A warm knowing smile appeared on Sigmund's face. "If you ask me if I think Benjy is here, the answer is yes."

"Really?" Kelsie was surprised.

"He loved this place. Why wouldn't he stay?"

"So, in your opinion, I shouldn't be afraid."

"Of Benjy?" Sigmund raised his eyebrows.

Kelsie felt silly. "Never mind."

Sigmund made a move to the cellar.

"Sig?"

"Yes?"

"Have you ever done a séance?"

Sigmund stood beside him to speak quietly. "You're determined to figure this mystery out?"

"I am. I dreamt about Benjy giving me permission to clear out the cellar, but I can't recall telling you."

"You wrote me a note."

Kelsie felt his skin prickle. "I did?"

"Yes. I found it on the counter in the kitchen."

"Can I see it?"

"I threw it away. I was certain it was from you."

"Did I sign it?"

"No. Was it from Marty? He didn't seem to be intimidated by the items we found."

"I don't think Marty would have made that request." Kelsie glanced at men coming and going, the exterminators. "Would you recognize Benjy's handwriting?"

"He wasn't a note writer. He used to just tell me what he needed."

"Okay." Kelsie didn't know what he expected to hear. But, for the life of him, he couldn't recall writing Sigmund a note. "Oh, about the séance?"

"I'll ask Helga. She likes those kinds of things." Sigmund laughed as if he were amused.

"Cool."

Sigmund patted his shoulder and headed down the ramp.

~

Marty used the treadmill, walking briskly, not running, hoping he could build up to an actual running program. He stared out of the window as he did, and held the rails. He was full from breakfast, but he wasn't going to let this room go to waste.

They did need music. Maybe a portable system.

"Hey."

Marty turned to look, seeing Kelsie enter the room.

"Good for you." Kelsie stood beside him.

"I have to start somewhere." Marty wasn't sweating yet.

Kelsie leaned back on the glass panes in front of the treadmill and crossed his arms. "Helga told me she's attended séances before."

"Are you serious about doing that?" Marty looked at the time left on his twenty minute program. "I'm more intimidated by a séance than I am the cellar."

"Marty?"

"Yeah?"

"Sigmund said I wrote him a note about the cellar."

"And?"

"I didn't."

"Are you sure?"

"Yes."

"Did you ask him to see it?" Marty felt the machine slowing as it went into a cool-down mode.

"I did ask. He threw it out."

Marty waited as the machine stopped. He stepped off, not feeling hot or even tired. He obviously didn't do much. "Did he recognize the handwriting?"

"You're asking the same questions I already asked."

"Huh. Well, that's a little odd."

Kelsie pulled him closer. "What if he's not dead?"

Marty narrowed his eyes at Kelsie. "Dude. He left us this place in his will."

"Did you see him sick?"

Marty thought about it. "He wouldn't let me see him."

"Me neither." Kelsie glanced at the doorway. "Do you know anyone who went to his funeral?"

"I assume Sig and Helga did."

"You assume? You said he was cremated. Who told you that?"

"I...I read it in the paper." Marty tried to recall. He scratched his head. "Didn't he have an obituary?"

"Would you put it passed Benjy to fake his death?"

"Why would he? That's absurd." Marty shook his head. "You're really letting this dream get to you."

"Think about it." Kelsie held Marty's shirt, preventing him from leaving the room. "Why did all those people come over here? Huh? If they knew Benjy had died, why would they still show up?"

Marty shook his head. "Dude. Wouldn't they have commented on the fact that the host wasn't even here?"

"They may have. I told you. I was blanked. No one talked to me."

"So, you think Benjy faked his death to leave us this place? Why? He could have just given it to us."

Kelsie seemed to ponder the facts.

"Let me change." Marty walked to the hallway, hearing Kelsie behind him. As they headed up to the second floor, Marty spotted the men from the pest-control company leaving, and the workers who were going to seal up the basement coming in with supplies.

Kelsie gestured to them. "And you somehow think I would make a command decision about that cellar? Me?"

"Why not? We own this place now." Marty made for his bedroom. Kelsie followed.

~

Kelsie sat on the foot of Marty's bed, still trying to wrap his head around how he had written a note. Maybe if he talked in his sleep, he also wrote in his sleep?

When Marty took off his gym shorts, Kelsie snapped out of his thoughts. He stared at Marty as he folded them neatly and dug through the drawers for something to wear.

"Marty?"

"Yeah?"

"Wanna make love?"

Marty turned to look at him from over his shoulder, then peered at the door to the room.

Kelsie stood up and locked it, then waited, not taking anything for granted.

~

Seeing the look of apprehension mixed with loneliness in Kelsie's green eyes, Marty softened up. He took off his T-shirt and then turned down the bed.

Kelsie's sad expression improved as he undressed and dropped his clothing onto the floor.

Marty removed the items they may need, placing them within reach. Kelsie crawled closer and relaxed next to him. Marty gave him a reassuring smile and cupped Kelsie's jaw over his soft facial hair.

They kissed and Marty drew Kelsie to lie over him. He spread his legs and bent his knees, cradling Kelsie.

Kelsie adjusted himself, resting his erection on Marty's. They hummed happily and ground against each other.

Marty parted from the kiss and stared into Kelsie's eyes. "This feels nice."

"It's about to feel a whole lot nicer." Kelsie braced himself up on his arms.

Marty rolled over, facing the bed, and got to his knees, his cheek against the soft pillow. As he waited for Kelsie to get ready, Marty had an image flash of Kelsie making love to Benjy. It wasn't a turn on, or off, but it was odd to imagine it right at this moment.

186

THE ODD COUPLE

All this talk of Benjy either being a ghost or not dead, was crazy. He chided himself for losing his concentration, as well as his erection and snapped back into focus when Kelsie ran his slick cock up and down his ass crack.

~

Kelsie stared at Marty's body, his pink-puckered rim and his tight butt. He pushed the head of his cock against it, and made his way beyond the tight ring of muscles. As Marty relaxed, letting go, Kelsie thought about making love to Benjy.

But, it wasn't lovemaking with Benjy. It was sex.

He adored Benjy, but not as a potential companion for life. Benjy was forty years older than he and Marty were.

Before he lost his erection from being distracted, Kelsie concentrated on what he was doing, but with the noise of the front door opening and closing, it wasn't easy.

~

Marty began to daydream, thinking about Benjy figuring out a way to give him and Kelsie the home, along with the promise of love and a potential lifetime partner.

Benjy could have just set them up on a date, right? He could have boasted about Kelsie, praised him, getting Marty interested in a blind date.

But, Marty had a feeling it wouldn't have worked. He never would have agreed.

No. This can't be an elaborate plan for Benjy to set us up. That's absurd.

When he heard Kelsie make a noise of frustration, Marty realized he had lost his erection too. He rolled over, and found Kelsie removing the condom.

"I hate these things." Kelsie dropped it on the nightstand. He flopped to his back and put one arm over his head while tugging on his dick.

Marty rolled to his side and stared at Kelsie. "I don't know about you, but I'm preoccupied as hell right now."

"I can always get it up." Kelsie kept tugging on himself.

"It's okay. We can snuggle."

"I keep wondering what the fuck Benjy did. Marty, when I was told we inherited his house, I was not only surprised, I was upset."

Marty could relate. He wished Benjy had at least mentioned something to him, if not about being his heir, about Kelsie.

Kelsie faced him. "Did Benjy tell you about me?"

"No."

"He didn't tell me about you either." Kelsie stopped playing with himself and tucked one hand under the pillow. "I hate mysteries and riddles."

"Maybe it was as simple as he liked us and thought we'd get along?"

"No. If he thought we'd get along, he'd have introduced us sooner, like when he was alive, and why would he attach all those restrictions on the terms." Kelsie rested one leg over Marty's thigh. "If we don't get along we can't have anything."

"Well…look at us. We're the odd couple."

"Are we?" Kelsie appeared as if he didn't buy it. "We may be different at first glance, but we're not that odd. As a matter of fact, I'm beginning to think we have more in common, than we have differences."

"Maybe he knew that." Marty touched Kelsie's shoulder. "He knew me well enough to know I wouldn't be into a fix-up."

Kelsie frowned. "He's really dead, isn't he?"

"Yeah. I think so. Getting into a hoax this elaborate? What would be the point? Just for us to meet? No. It doesn't make sense."

"Damn." Kelsie rolled to his back.

THE ODD COUPLE

"It's okay. We'll manage." Marty kissed Kelsie's chest and smoothed his hand down to his crotch, cupping Kelsie's soft cock and balls.

~

Kelsie urged Marty into his arms and held onto him.

Maybe Benjy knew he needed a lifeline. If Benjy had gotten ill and was aware he was going to die, he was one hell of a friend to do what he had done.

If Kelsie had been left on the street without Benjy's help, no doubt he would have slid into a further depression.

And the two of them had one thing in common for certain; their cell-phones never made a sound.

Kelsie fell asleep in Marty's arms.

As their foreplay melted away to slumber, Kelsie floated on a dream.

~

Marty nodded off until he heard Kelsie talking.

He became lucid but didn't move.

"…I know…it was scary."

Marty raised his head off the pillow to see if someone else was in the room. There wasn't anyone else here.

"…only if you say so…"

"Kelsie?" Marty nudged his shoulder.

"Bye, Benj."

"Kel?" Marty shook him to wake him.

Kelsie opened his eyes. "What?"

"You were talking in your sleep again."

"I was?" Kelsie rubbed his face and yawned. "What time is it?"

"Do you remember the dream?" Marty leaned on his elbow, propping up his chin.

"No. What did I say?"

"You sounded as if you were talking to Benjy. You even said his name."

Kelsie went limp while lying on his back, staring into space. "We need a séance."

"Okay." Marty shrugged.

When Kelsie sat up and placed his feet on the floor, Marty did as well. Feeling groggy from the nap, Marty splashed his face at the sink to wake up. He imagined Kelsie joining him to do the same, but when he peeked into the bedroom, Kelsie had left.

~

Kelsie didn't hear men's voices in the house any longer. He walked the length of the first floor to the basement door. The drop cloths had been removed and the carpets vacuumed.

He tugged on the basement door, and it was indeed latched. He went in search of Helga.

He found her in the kitchen, preparing coleslaw and potato salad.

"Are you hungry?" she asked him.

"A little. Helga?"

"Yes?" She dried her hands and then stirred the sliced red potatoes with a wooden spoon.

"Can we do a séance together?"

She paused in her preparation and gazed at him. "What do you hope to achieve?"

"I want to know if he's here."

"Don't you already know that?"

"Please?"

She appeared to think about it. "I have a friend who claims to be psychic."

Kelsie leaned against the counter as he paid attention.

"I can see if she's available. To be honest, Kelsie, I'm not interested in being a part of it."

"I understand." He was about to leave her to her work, when he asked, "Did you read the note I wrote for Sigmund?"

"No. He just told me about it. Why?"

"Never mind." He picked up an apple from a bowl and rubbed it on his shirt. "Let me know when your friend can come by."

"I'll text her now." Helga picked up her phone from the counter.

Kelsie bit into the apple, staring at the spotless kitchen.

Marty stepped into the room. "Are we eating again?"

Kelsie finished chewing. "I don't know."

"I'm not hungry yet. I'm still full from before." Marty rubbed his belly and looked at the salad bowls. "Man, that looks good. Are we having a barbecue again?"

Helga read her phone and then said, "She's willing to do it for you."

"Who's willing to do what?" Marty used a clean fork to taste the potato salad.

"A friend of Helga's is going to do a séance with us."

Marty stopped chewing and his eyes went wide.

"When?" Kelsie asked.

"She's free tonight. She said the later in the evening the better."

"Uh-oh." Marty set the fork into the sink. "Should we do this?"

Helga held her phone in her hand. "Kelsie?"

"Yes."

Her thumbs moved over the keypad of her phone. "Okay. She's coming by tonight at ten."

Marty asked, "Will you and Sigmund be joining us?"

"No. I'm not comfortable doing that here." She set her phone aside, and opened the refrigerator.

191

Finishing his apple and tossing the core, Kelsie watched as she took marinated pork ribs out and set it on the counter. He tapped Marty and gestured for him to leave the kitchen with him.

Marty did, and they left through the back slider and stood near the pool.

"I know it's scary," Kelsie said, "But, don't you want answers?"

"I don't know what the questions are."

"*Are you dead?* would be a good beginning."

"Kel." Marty narrowed his eyes at him.

Kelsie held up his hand to stop the expected chiding. "After tonight, I won't discuss it again."

"Okay." Marty walked away, stopping to smell the roses.

Chapter 18

After a dinner of barbecued ribs, coleslaw and potato salad, Helga and Sigmund cleaned up the kitchen and grill, and left.

Marty wandered the house alone, and was drawn to the room with the cellar door in it. Helga had set up a folding table, and three chairs were at three sides. The table had a black cloth covering it, and two candles were set in simple sticks, matches near them.

Marty wasn't sure what he thought about this idea, but if it gave Kelsie closure and he could move on, it was worth it.

He touched the door to the cellar, and closed his eyes. Since it had been cleared out, and the mice exterminated, Marty saw no reason to seal it up. After all, when they died, and this place was once again on the market, wouldn't the new occupants wonder why this area had been sealed?

They would no doubt open it up to inspect. He would.

He sighed and glanced at the hallway, seeing it growing dark with the evening hours.

He was about to look for Kelsie when he heard a light clicking noise.

Marty paused to listen.

The door to the cellar was rattling.

He touched the handle, shaking it. Wind would certainly make it move.

Now I'm letting him get to me. He shook his head at his own thoughts and left the room.

~

On his knees, Kelsie rummaged through Benjy's closet. He opened the plastic bins and tossed feather boas, wigs and high heeled shoes onto the floor beside him.

Heating up from the effort, Kelsie brushed the hair back from his forehead and took a deep breath. "If you're here, buddy, now's the time to let me know what you're thinking." He looked around the closet at the hanging clothing.

"I mean it, Benjy."

"Kel?"

Kelsie jumped out of his skin and held his chest.

"Sorry. What are you doing?"

"I was trying to get an outfit together." He held up a rainbow colored boa.

"For…you?"

"Yes. For me." He managed to get to his feet, even with pins and needles in his legs from kneeling. He wrapped the boa around his neck. "I figured it would help."

"Helga set up a card table."

"Cool." Kelsie wedged his foot into a high heeled shoe.

"It's in the room where the door to the cellar is."

Kelsie wobbled on the footwear and held onto Marty's shoulder for balance. "Well, that's a scary spot. Where else would we do it?" He put his second foot into the other shoe.

"Why not here?"

Kelsie immediately met Marty's gaze. "No! No way."

"Are you sure? His bedroom, his closet, his stuff?"

"Dude! No! I can close that room off and never see it again. I can't do that here." He tried to walk in the high-heels and struggled, his ankles turning. "How did he balance on these?"

"Practice." Marty held onto Kelsie to keep him upright. "I'm going to the game room to read until she comes."

"Okay. I'll meet you there."

Marty released his hold on Kelsie. "Got it?"

THE ODD COUPLE

Kelsie stood still. "Got it."

Marty left the closet and the second he did, Kelsie's foot tilted on the heel and he fell to the carpeted floor. He blew the feathers off his face and sighed.

~

Marty curled up in his favorite chair, his e-reader on his lap. Since he loved to read, he became lost in the story.

He looked up when Kelsie entered. Kelsie was wearing one of Benjy's drag outfits, a gold lame jumpsuit, which was large on him, a rainbow feather boa, plastic bangles and beads, pink hoop earrings, a blonde wig and platform shoes.

Marty bit his lip on his laughter, but when Kelsie spit out feathers from his lips, Marty lost it. He roared with hilarity and dabbed at his eyes.

"No?" Kelsie looked down at himself.

"Holy shit." Marty couldn't stop laughing, nearly falling off the chair.

Kelsie perked up. "That's the doorbell." He held the wall and managed to walk away.

Marty took a few deep breaths to calm down. He shut off the e-reader, set it on the chair, and jogged to the front door.

~

Kelsie carefully made his way on the high shoes. He flipped the boa behind his shoulder, blew out the feathers stuck to his mouth, and opened the door.

The woman standing on his stoop's eyes widened in surprise.

"Lulu?" he asked, opening the screen door for her.

"Yes." The robust older woman wearing a red turban made a deliberate appraisal of his outfit. "Benjy's clothing?"

"Did you know him" Kelsie touched the gold lame.

"Of course. Everyone knew Benjy." She adjusted the strap of a large purse over her shoulder and entered the home.

"You must be Kelsie." She shook his hand.

"I am." He managed to close the door behind her, and stay upright.

Marty approached her, hand extended. "I'm Marty Hayes."

"Nice to meet you." She shook it.

Kelsie grabbed onto Marty as he tried to walk. "We set up a place near the creepy basement."

"Why are you dressed like that?" she asked as Marty held Kelsie upright.

"I thought it would bring him closer to me."

Marty didn't add his two cents, and Kelsie was grateful. "Let me show you the way."

Lulu said, "I know the way."

Marty and Kelsie exchanged glances and shrugged.

"Would you like anything to drink?" Marty asked as Lulu walked down the hallway.

"Maybe after."

Marty stared at Kelsie. "After?"

"Works for me." Kelsie gripped Marty firmly and the two of them headed down the hall.

~

Once Marty helped Kelsie to walk to the room, he realized Lulu had placed objects on the card table.

A spirit board with its planchette, crystals, a deck of tarot cards and a small recording device.

"Shut off the light, please."

Marty closed the door to the room and turned off the light. Lulu lit the three candles that Helga had placed on the table.

Kelsie sat on one side of Lulu, and he took the chair opposite Kelsie.

Lulu blew out the match and passed her hands over the flames, muttering under her breath. She relaxed in the folding chair and rested both of her hands on the table near the board.

"Helga explained to me you were seeking answers as to whether Benjy is still here."

Marty felt a chill up his spine but didn't tell the other two.

"Yes." Kelsie flipped the boa behind his shoulder and brushed the blonde wig's hair from his face. "I know he's here. I mean. He's really here."

Marty wondered if this was going to freak Kelsie out more than it was going to offer comfort.

"What I want to ask him is if he's the one who told Sigmund to seal up...that room." Kelsie pointed to it and exaggerated his shudder of fear.

"The cellar?" Lulu asked. "He enjoyed collecting wine."

Marty became intrigued. "How well did you know Benjy?"

"We were connected spiritually. I knew him as a close friend."

Marty and Kelsie exchanged glances.

Before Marty could get out a word, Kelsie asked her, "Why did he leave the house to me and Marty?"

"He loved you."

Marty blinked. "He told you that?"

"He didn't have to. Don't his actions speak for him?"

"Whoa." Kelsie shifted on the chair. "Then, he did die?"

Marty didn't want Lulu to think they were ungrateful, or worse, crazy. "We know he died—"

"Death isn't an end. It's a beginning." Lulu shifted the Ouija board closer to the middle of the table.

An invisible breeze made Marty tingle. He looked around the room, but the windows and doors were closed, and the air conditioning was not on.

The candle flames danced in the moving air.

"Let's open the spirit door, shall we?" Lulu reached out her hands.

Marty clasped one of hers, and one of Kelsie's. He'd seen enough TV shows that used these spirit boards to know they had to invite the dead in first.

Kelsie's hand was ice cold, obviously showing how nervous he was.

Lulu closed her eyes and initiated the séance.

"We welcome you to the light. Come join us. Benjy Lloyd, we call upon you to bring comfort. Show these men you loved you are not suffering."

More chills rushed up Marty's spine, but he was convinced it was the 'creep-out' sensation from his own mind.

"We open up a portal to the other side, inviting good spirits only. Negative entities are banned from entering."

Kelsie squeezed Marty's hand tightly.

Marty peeked across the table at him. Marty was the only one with his eyes open.

"Benjy Lloyd, come to us. Come back from the other side to communicate to your loved ones."

Marty felt Lulu release his fingers. He sat up straighter and tried not to become frightened.

Lulu touched the planchette. "Who will ask Benjy questions with me?"

Marty tucked his hands under his legs. "He is."

Kelsie nodded, biting his lower lip.

"Please rest your hands palms down on the table."

Marty did, pressing his fingers flat.

"Kelsie." She indicated the Ouija board.

Kelsie blew out a few loud breaths, shook his hands off and then rested his fingertips on top of the planchette.

"Don't add any pressure to it. Allow it to move." Lulu rested her fingers on it too.

Marty felt his stomach tighten in apprehension.

"Benjy Lloyd," she began, "Your light continues to shine on these young men. Show them you are here."

The candles bent and flickered.

"Whoa." Kelsie exaggerated his shiver.

"Ask a question, Kelsie." Lulu waited.

"Um...Benj?" Kelsie looked up at the ceiling. "Is it okay if I seal up the basement?"

Marty kept his focus on the candle flames, which weren't moving at the moment. As Marty detected a shift in the electromagnetic static in the air, both of their hands moved across the board to, 'No.'

Lulu voiced the answer, "No, Benjy?"

Their hands swung across the board, and back to the word, 'No.'

"You're moving that!" Kelsie accused.

"Kel, she's barely touching it."

Lulu closed her eyes. "You do not wish them to seal the basement door? Yes to seal it, no, not to."

Marty tried to see if Lulu was indeed moving the planchette. Her hands were limp on the object and when it moved, her muscles didn't flex.

Once more it read, 'No.'

"Benjy," Lulu said, "Do you want these boys to be happy in your home?"

Marty's skin broke out in goose bumps.

The planchette swung to the word, 'Yes.'

Marty seriously doubted a spirit was doing that. Lulu had to be.

As if she sensed his suspicions, Lulu took her hands off the planchette. "Marty, rest your fingers on it."

Kelsie stared at him, communicating for him to do just that.

Since he had to see this for himself, Marty did, resting his fingers so lightly on the planchette, he would know if Kelsie moved it.

"Ask a question," Lulu whispered.

Kelsie made a face of fear at him.

Marty cleared his throat. "Benjy? Um...is there any reason we should be afraid of the basement?" He waited, watching the board.

The planchette didn't budge. Just as he became convinced Lulu had indeed moved it, it rolled to the word, 'No.'

"You did that." Marty watched Kelsie.

"Nope." He shook his head adamantly.

"Benjy? Are you answering us or is it just us?"

Lulu said, "One question at a time."

Kelsie repeated, "Benjy? Are you moving this thing?"

Marty made sure he was barely touching the planchette. It rolled to 'Yes.'

He retracted his hands in shock.

Lulu reached for their hands once more. They clasped them.

Now Kelsie's fingers were not only cold, they were clammy.

"Benjy...what do you wish for these men?"

Marty wondered how he would answer, since they weren't using the board anymore.

Kelsie became animated. "Dahhling! I want you to love each other."

Marty narrowed his eyes at Kelsie in annoyance.

Lulu perked up. "Benjy, why did you leave the house to Kelsie and Marty?"

"Lonely, lonely men. I wanted them to find each other."

Marty was about to kick Kelsie under the table to get him to stop.

Kelsie had his eyes closed and his hand warmed.

"I loved, and loved, but couldn't find the true love."

Marty watched Kelsie's face in the candlelight. His eyes were moving under his closed eyelids.

"What is it you want to tell them, Benjy?"

"As long as you hold onto each other, you have nothing to fear."

The hairs were standing on Marty's neck. He became icy cold. Then it occurred to him, Kelsie didn't sound like he was impersonating Benjy, he sounded like the man himself.

No. No way.

"Love is the answer. There isn't a fear it can't cure."

"Kel?" Marty whispered.

Lulu squeezed Marty's hand to stop him from ruining the moment. "Benjy, these men miss you very much."

Marty's eyes filled with tears instantly.

"I'm here. I will be here until they find their way."

Marty wasn't pleased with the charade. He pulled both hands back and folded his arms. He became convinced Kelsie and Lulu had concocted this act.

Kelsie opened his eyes. "What's wrong?"

"We need to close the séance." Lulu reached out to Marty.

Marty humored her, but he was furious.

"Let the portal close. No spirits can enter uninvited. If you have come to the light, you may leave with it. Be at peace."

~

Kelsie had no idea why Marty looked annoyed. He also wished something had actually happened to them. Not seeing any sign of Benjy was disappointing. But, what did he expect from a psychic with a spirit board?

"The circle is now closed." Lulu blew out the candles and released their hands.

Kelsie waited until Marty turned on a light. "Oh, well." Kelsie removed the boa from his neck and the wig from his head. "Better luck next time."

"Huh?" Marty stood near the table. "What do you mean?"

"I mean, nothing happened." Kelsie folded his arms.

Lulu picked up the recorder and pushed a button.

Kelsie hadn't noticed she'd had one. He held a crystal and inspected it.

Lulu set the recorder near him, and hit play.

Marty sat back down, and he was staring at him with so much intensity Kelsie became confused.

"Dahhling! I want you to love each other."

Kelsie tilted his head at Marty. "When did you tape that?"

"Benjy, why did you leave the house to Kelsie and Marty?"

"Lonely, lonely men. I wanted them to find each other."

Kelsie was about to make another snide comment about when this conversation was recorded, when he could see Marty appeared pale.

"Did that voice come through just now?" Kelsie asked.

"You don't remember it?" Marty asked.

"I loved, and loved, but couldn't find the true love."

"What is it you want to tell them, Benjy?"

"As long as you hold onto each other, you have nothing to fear."

"Is that me?" Kelsie felt as if he were on the verge of a panic attack.

Lulu stopped the recording. "That was you channeling Benjy."

About to laugh and say how stupid that was, Kelsie looked at Marty. He wasn't amused.

"Dude." He tried to make light of it. "I mimic him all the time."

"Kel, you weren't mimicking him. If you did, wouldn't you remember?"

THE ODD COUPLE

A chill as cold as ice passed over him. Kelsie managed to get to his feet, and staggered on the platform shoes. He yanked them off and ran all the way up to his room.

~

Marty watched him go in amazement.

Lulu collected her crystals and cards, and put the board back into her purse. She took the recorder with her.

"What now?" Marty asked.

"He loves you both. He only wants you to be happy."

"He told us not to seal up the basement."

"He did. But, it's now up to you two." Lulu stood and held her purse on her shoulder. "I also do cleansing. Let me know if you need it."

"Huh?" Marty was still trying to figure out how Kelsie did what he had done.

"I can find my way out."

Marty stood up and shook her hand. He took a moment to gather his thoughts and ended up staring at the door to the cellar.

~

Kelsie removed the jumpsuit and boa, throwing them into the closet. He crawled over the bed and burrowed underneath the blankets, hiding.

"Dude!" He shivered. "Did ya have to freak me out?"

When he felt the bed shift, Kelsie screamed.

"Kelsie! It's me!"

He batted his way out of the sheet and saw Marty sitting on the bed.

Kelsie clung onto him and hid his face.

"So, for real? That wasn't you pretending?"

"Dude! I don't even remember saying that shit."

"Maybe it's a form of hypnosis."

Kelsie rested his head on Marty's shoulder. "Whatever it was, I have no recollection of saying anything like that."

203

"Well, if it was legit, then we got Benjy's opinion on the cellar."

"What was it?"

"He doesn't want it sealed up."

"Damn." Kelsie squeezed Marty closer.

"You wanted to ask." Marty put his arm around him.

"I did." Kelsie took comfort in Marty's warmth. "Okay. Benjy gets the last word."

"He does."

Kelsie leaned back to see into Marty's eyes. "I'm not alone anymore."

The smile on Marty's face was pure comfort. "No. Neither am I." He caressed Kelsie's face and kissed him.

~

Marty woke in the night. He and Kelsie had fallen asleep in the master bedroom. As he was about to roll over and try to drift off once more, Marty noticed someone standing at the foot of the bed.

Benjy was there, smiling at him.

Marty smiled back.

"Are you happy, dahhling?"

"I am, Benjy. Thank you."

"Take care of each other."

"We will."

~

Kelsie heard someone talking. He opened his eyes and checked on Marty. Marty was sound asleep, smiling about something, maybe a dream.

Kelsie was about to close his eyes and return to slumber when he heard Marty say, "We're not the odd couple...we're the right couple."

Kelsie took a look around the dim room. Nothing was amiss. He snuggled against Marty, pulling him close.

"Do you love me?"

Kelsie stared at Marty's expression. He seemed to be talking in his sleep. "Do I love you?"

"Yes."

"You know I do."

Marty's expression became passive and he let go a soft sigh.

Kelsie held him tight, staring into the dark room.

And then...

"The next item for auction...an extremely rare 1923 ACE motorcycle...it's all original, original paint...including the blue tank with its eagle decal still intact...All proceeds from this sale will be donated to charity. We have a lot of phone bids on this...so let's start the bidding at twenty-thousand...twenty, twenty- do I hear twenty-five?

"I have thirty...forty...forty...I have fifty! On the phone, fifty thousand...do I hear sixty?" The auctioneer pointed his gavel. "I have sixty, seventy? Seventy...I have seventy, the man in the front row...eighty? Do I have eighty?

"Eighty...do I have ninety thousand?...Eighty to the bidder on the phone...eighty, do I have eighty-one? No? Last bid? Eighty? Anyone left on the phone? Final chance! Going once, going twice...eighty-thousand dollars!"

Applause rang out and Kelsie and Marty screamed in excitement, both dressed in colorful clothing with feather boas around their necks. They did a happy dance and hopped up and down.

A few hours later, back home, Kelsie strummed his guitar, humming a melody.

Marty reclined on a lounge chair reading.

The sun was bright, not a cloud was in the sky, and the scent of roses filled the air.

Helga opened the glass sliding door and brought out a tray to them.

Kelsie perked up and set his guitar aside.

A pitcher with an exotic fruit drink, complete with strawberries, pineapple, and mango, were sliced and on the swizzle stick. Beside the drink were snacks, crackers, cheese, olives, and nuts.

"Thank you, Helga." Marty smiled at her.

"You're very welcome. This came for you in the mail." She held up a letter.

Kelsie glanced at Marty to see if he was going to read it, but he picked up a wedge of cheese and ate it.

Kelsie reached for the letter, seeing it had come from the lawyer's office.

Helga went back into the house as he unsealed it and pulled the contents out of the envelope.

Marty brushed off his hands and asked, "Is it bad news? Those things are always bad news."

Kelsie read it, then looked at Marty. "Um. It's from the estate lawyer. She's asking if we're still together."

Marty poured them both a drink from the pitcher. "Well. We are. Now what?"

Kelsie kept reading. The letter reminded them in order to continue living at the house, they had to submit proof they were a couple. Kelsie narrowed his eyes and asked, "How are we supposed to do that?"

"Do what?" Marty ate his fruit off the swizzle stick.

"The terms of our agreement state we have to submit proof that we're in love."

"Do they want a sex tape?" Marty smiled.

Kelsie touched the letter to his lip as he thought about it. "That's one idea. I have another."

"What's that?" Marty scooted onto Kelsie's lounge chair and rested on his lap.

"Marry me?"

Marty laughed and then stared into his eyes. "For real?"

Kelsie handed him the letter. As Marty read if for himself, Kelsie cupped Marty's cheek in his palm and admired him.

"Huh. I guess Benjy was serious about the two of us being a permanent couple." He set the letter on the patio and relaxed on top of Kelsie.

"So?"

"It hasn't been very long."

"Is that a no?"

Marty inched his way higher and kissed him. "That's a yes."

Kelsie pumped his fist into the air. "Thank you, Benjy!"

Marty straddled Kelsie's legs and pressed their crotches together. They made happy noises as they kissed.

Then, while Kelsie couldn't believe how lucky he was, Marty started to laugh against Kelsie's mouth.

Kelsie met his gaze and they cracked up with hilarity. "Can I make love to you here on the patio?"

"Yup." Marty answered, tongue in cheek.

They began to shimmy out of their clothing excitedly.

Once they were naked, Kelsie bent his knees and spread his legs, allowing Marty to lie between them.

Swirling tongues, making lovesick noises, the two of them heated up. As the grinding friction of their hard cocks lit them up, Kelsie parted from the kisses to breathe deeply.

Marty inched lower to suck his cock.

Kelsie dug his fingers into Marty's hair as he took his length into his mouth. "Oh, yes."

"Mmm." Marty hummed as he sucked.

Kelsie unwound and relaxed, letting it build. As Marty bobbed up and down on his dick, Kelsie watched. A red feather fell from the heavens, landing on his chest.

They both watched it; Marty holding Kelsie's cock still in his mouth, and Kelsie trying not to gasp in surprise.

It rested on Kelsie's abdomen, right in front of Marty's nose. He released his suction from Kelsie's cock and stared at it.

Kelsie picked it up carefully, inspecting it. "That's odd."

THE ODD COUPLE

Marty craned his neck to the sky and then the surroundings. "Maybe not, Kel. I'm beginning to think there's nothing odd about any of this."

Kelsie set the tiny feather under his guitar strings. "Yeah. Maybe you're right. There's no such thing as an odd couple, is there?"

"Nope." Marty reached for a kiss and Kelsie hugged him tight.

Dahhling! You're so in love! You are loved and loved and loved! And I just love a happy ending.

The End

About the Author

Author G.A. Hauser is from Fair Lawn, New Jersey, USA. She attended university at The Fashion Institute of Technology in NYC, and has a BA in Fine Art from William Paterson College in Wayne NJ where she graduated Cum Laude. As well as degrees in art, G.A. is a Graduate Gemologist from the Gemological Institute of America (GIA). In 1994 G.A. graduated the Washington State Police academy as a Peace Officer for the Seattle Police Department in Washington where she worked on the patrol division. She was awarded Officer of the Month in February 2000 for her work with recovering stolen vehicles and fingerprint matches to auto-theft and bank robbery suspects. After working for the Seattle Police, G.A. moved to Hertfordshire, England where she began to write full length gay romance novels. Now a full-time writer, G.A. has penned over 150 novels and short stories. Breaking into independent film, G. A. was the executive producer for her first feature film, CAPITAL GAMES which included TV star Shane Keough in its cast. CAPITAL GAMES had its Film Festival Premiere at Philly's Qfest, and its television premiere on OutTV. G.A. is the director and executive producer for her second film NAKED DRAGON, which is an interracial gay police/FBI drama filmed in Los Angeles with the outstanding cinematographer, Pete Borosh. (also the Cinematographer for Capital Games)

The cover photographs of G.A.'s novels have been selected from talented and prolific photographers such as Dennis Dean, Dan Skinner, Michael Stokes, Tuta Veloso, Hans Withoos, and CJC Photography, as well as graphic comic artist, Arlen Schumer. Her cover designs have featured actors Chris Salvatore, Jeffery Patrick Olson, Tom Wolfe, and models Brian James Bradley, Bryan Feiss, Jimmy Thomas, Andre Flagger, Grigoris Drakakis, among many others.

Her advertisements have been printed in Attitude Magazine, LA Frontiers, and Gay Times.

G. A. has won awards from All Romance eBooks for Best Author 2009, Best Novel 2008, *Mile High*, Best Author 2008, Best Novel 2007, *Secrets and Misdemeanors*, and Best Author 2007.

G.A. was the guest speaker at the SLA conference in San Diego, in 2013, where she discussed women writing gay erotica and has attended numerous writers' conventions across the country.

THE ODD COUPLE

The G.A. Hauser Collection
FEATURE FILMS

NAKED DRAGON

CAPITAL GAMES

Single Titles

Unnecessary Roughness

Hot Rod

Mr. Right

Happy Endings

Down and Dirty

Lancelot in Love

Midnight in London

Living Dangerously

The Last Hard Man

Taking Ryan

Born to be Wilde

Boys

Band of Brothers

I Love You I Hate You

Marry Me

G. A. HAUSER

The Farmer's Son

One Two Three

Three Wishes

Bedtime Stories

The Reunion

The Ugly Truth

I'd Kill For You

Snapped

What Happens in Vegas…

Aroused and Awakened

Trent is a Slut

My Super Boyfriend

Lost

From A to Zeke

Whether or Not

Bound to You

Lover Boy

The Fall of Rome

Along Comes a Man

A Matter of Minutes

Away and Back

THE ODD COUPLE

Gay for Pay

Cry Like an Angel

I'll Say I'm Sorry Now

Venetian Blue

Ghost Hunter

Someone Like You

I Don't Know Why

The Prom Date

Jealousy

Something to Believe in

Showboys

These Four Walls

Between a Rock & a Hard Place

The Odd Couple

My Best Friend's Boyfriend

The Diamond Stud

The Hard Way

Games Men Play

Born to Please

Got Men?

Heart of Steele

G. A. HAUSER

All Man

Julian

In The Dark and What Should Never Be

A Man's Best Friend

Blind Ambition

For Love and Money

The Kiss

Secrets and Misdemeanors

To Have and To Hostage

The Boy Next Door

Exposure

Murphy's Hero

Calling Dr Love

The Rape of St. Peter

The Wedding Planner

Going Deep

Teacher's Pet

Historic Books

Mark Antonious deMontford

Pirates

In the Shadow of Alexander

The Rise and Fall of the Sacred Band of Thebes

Cowboy Books

Cowboy Blues

Rough Ride

Hardcore Houston

Save a Horse…

Interracial Books

Miller's Tale

Naked Dragon

Code Red

It Takes a Man

Paranormal/Vampire Books

The Vampire and the Man-eater

Lie With Me

Vampire Nights

London, Bloody, London

Dude! Did You Just Bite Me?

Giving Up the Ghost

Black Leather Phoenix

Fantasy Books

The Adonis of WeHo

Prince of Servitude

Timeless (Sci-Fi)

THE ODD COUPLE

The Action! Series

Acting Naughty

Playing Dirty

Getting it in the End

Behaving Badly

Dripping Hot

Packing Heat

Being Screwed

Something Sexy

Going Wild

Having it All!

Bending the Rules

Keeping it Up

Making Love

Staying Power

Saying Goodbye

Coming Home

Knowing Better

Becoming Alex

Doing the Dirty

Anything But

Mark & Billy

Changing Times

Mark Antonious Richfield

Obsession

G. A. HAUSER

L.A. Masquerade

Prequels & related books for The Action Series
Capital Games

Mark and Sharon

Miller's Tale

COPS

Double Trouble

Love you, Loveday

When Adam Met Jack

(The **Heroes Series***)*

Military Men
Bound to You

It Takes a Man

All Man

I'd Kill For You

Living Dangerously

The Last Hard Man

Happy Endings

THE ODD COUPLE

Men in Motion Series

Mile High

Cruising

Driving Hard

Leather Boys

Heroes Series (Men in Uniform)

Man to Man

Two In Two Out

Top Men

Wolf Shifter Series

Of Wolves and Men

The Order of Wolves

Among Wolves

G.A. Hauser

Writing as Amanda Winters

Sister Moonshine

Nothing Like Romance

Silent Reign

Butterfly Suicide

Mutley's Crew

Orion in the Sky

Free Reads!

(available through my website)

Dude! Did You Just Bite Me?

L.A. Masquerade

Lie With Me

Exchange of Hearts

Live, Love...Last

Strangers With Candy

Dark Angel

Made in the USA
Middletown, DE
24 April 2018